Longarm crouched and
alcove. He saw two bushwhackers running across the street toward him. Muzzle flame jetted at him, and a slug chewed splinters from the wall above his head. He fired and saw one of the men go over backward as if a giant fist had just smashed into him. The other man fired wildly, the bullets shattering a window to Longarm's right. He took his time coolly lining up the shot and pulled the Colt's trigger again. This slug ripped through the second man's body and spun him off his feet.

Shouts came from down the street. For the third time this evening, what sounded like a small-scale war had broken out in Warhorse . . . and the night was still young.

DON'T MISS THESE
ALL-ACTION WESTERN SERIES
FROM THE BERKLEY PUBLISHING GROUP

THE GUNSMITH by J. R. Roberts
Clint Adams was a legend among lawmen, outlaws, and ladies. They called him . . . the Gunsmith.

LONGARM by Tabor Evans
The popular long-running series about Deputy U.S. Marshal Custis Long—his life, his loves, his fight for justice.

SLOCUM by Jake Logan
Today's longest-running action Western. John Slocum rides a deadly trail of hot blood and cold steel.

BUSHWHACKERS by B. J. Lanagan
An action-packed series by the creators of Longarm! The rousing adventures of the most brutal gang of cutthroats ever assembled—Quantrill's Raiders.

DIAMONDBACK by Guy Brewer
Dex Yancey is Diamondback, a Southern gentleman turned con man when his brother cheats him out of the family fortune. Ladies love him. Gamblers hate him. But nobody pulls one over on Dex . . .

WILDGUN by Jack Hanson
The blazing adventures of mountain man Will Barlow— from the creators of Longarm!

TEXAS TRACKER by Tom Calhoun
J.T. Law: the most relentless—and dangerous—manhunter in all Texas. Where sheriffs and posses fail, he's the best man to bring in the most vicious outlaws—for a price.

TABOR EVANS

LONGARM

AND THE DEADLY FLOOD

JOVE BOOKS, NEW YORK

THE BERKLEY PUBLISHING GROUP
Published by the Penguin Group
Penguin Group (USA) Inc.
375 Hudson Street, New York, New York 10014, USA
Penguin Group (Canada), 90 Eglinton Avenue East, Suite 700, Toronto, Ontario M4P 2Y3, Canada
(a division of Pearson Penguin Canada Inc.)
Penguin Books Ltd., 80 Strand, London WC2R 0RL, England
Penguin Group Ireland, 25 St. Stephen's Green, Dublin 2, Ireland (a division of Penguin Books Ltd.)
Penguin Group (Australia), 250 Camberwell Road, Camberwell, Victoria 3124, Australia
(a division of Pearson Australia Group Pty. Ltd.)
Penguin Books India Pvt. Ltd., 11 Community Centre, Panchsheel Park, New Delhi—110 017, India
Penguin Group (NZ), 67 Apollo Drive, Rosedale, North Shore 0632, New Zealand
(a division of Pearson New Zealand Ltd.)
Penguin Books (South Africa) (Pty.) Ltd., 24 Sturdee Avenue, Rosebank, Johannesburg 2196,
South Africa

Penguin Books Ltd., Registered Offices: 80 Strand, London WC2R 0RL, England

This is a work of fiction. Names, characters, places, and incidents either are the product of the author's imagination or are used fictitiously, and any resemblance to actual persons, living or dead, business establishments, events, or locales is entirely coincidental.

LONGARM AND THE DEADLY FLOOD

A Jove Book / published by arrangement with the author

PRINTING HISTORY
Jove edition / June 2010

Copyright © 2010 by Penguin Group (USA) Inc.
Cover illustration by Miro Sinovcic.

ISBN: 978-0-515-14810-7

JOVE®
Jove Books are published by The Berkley Publishing Group,
a division of Penguin Group (USA) Inc.,
375 Hudson Street, New York, New York 10014.
JOVE® is a registered trademark of Penguin Group (USA) Inc.
The "J" design is a trademark of Penguin Group (USA) Inc.

PRINTED IN THE UNITED STATES OF AMERICA

10 9 8 7 6 5 4 3 2 1

Chapter 1

The sky was leaden with rain as Longarm rode toward the town of Warhorse in Arizona Territory, but the drops hadn't started falling yet. Static electricity crackled in the air and sparks seemed to dance around the tips of his horse's ears. The smell of rain filled the air as the animal's hooves clomped heavily across the wooden bridge spanning the dry wash that curved around the town and ran into another arroyo about half a mile east of the settlement.

Longarm didn't like it.

He fished out the turnip watch that he carried in one pocket of his vest and flipped it open. As he'd thought, the time was only a little after four o'clock in the afternoon. There ought to be about four hours of sunlight left at this season of the year. Instead, the sky was so dark that it seemed like night was about to fall.

The looming bulk of Warhorse Mountain just to the west of town didn't help matters. It was a black, ugly mountain that went almost straight up, rising to a jagged peak that somebody in the past thought resembled the silhouette of a charging horse. That had given the mountain its name, and the town was named after the mountain.

Longarm had never been here before, but he had heard of the place. There were ranches to the east and mines in the rugged mountain range to the west, none of them too successful. Warhorse served as the supply center for both industries, which meant it had several general stores, a blacksmith shop and livery stable, a few assorted other businesses, and more saloons than anything else. It was hard to go broke providing booze and whores to cowboys and miners, although of course some luckless—or stupid—hombres managed to do just that.

Longarm didn't care about any of that. He just wanted to find Ed Galloway, arrest the son of a bitchin' outlaw, and get out of this backwater burg. It was a day and a half ride back to Phoenix, where he'd get on a train bound for Denver with his prisoner.

Once they reached Denver, he'd turn the murdering bastard over to the federal court, which would try, convict, sentence, and then hang Ed Galloway. Murder was a state crime, but robbing a train full of gold bullion on its way to the mint to be struck into coins put the matter in Uncle Sam's hands. Longarm didn't care who officially pulled the lever on the gallows, as long as Galloway's neck got stretched good and proper.

Galloway had killed the conductor on that train . . . and the conductor had been Longarm's friend.

The big lawman reached the end of the bridge. The sun had been shining when he broke camp that morning, but clouds had rolled in steadily during the day. Storms were rare in this part of the country, but when they occurred, they were usually humdingers. Chances were, he wouldn't be able to start back today, which meant he'd have to lock Galloway up for the night here in Warhorse.

According to what he'd been told by the local law back in Phoenix, there was a town marshal charged with keeping the peace in Warhorse, so he'd likely have an office and a small jail. Longarm hoped it was sturdy enough to hold a desperate owlhoot like Galloway. If not, he'd lock the varmint up in a smokehouse or something.

Thunder rumbled in the distance. Fingers of lightning clawed through the black sky over Warhorse Mountain. Longarm heaved a sigh. The weather just wasn't going to cooperate with him.

"Mister! Hey, mister!"

Longarm looked to his left, saw that a kid in overalls and a scrawny brown-and-tan dog had run up alongside him. He reined the horse he had rented in Phoenix to a halt and gave the boy a nod.

"Howdy, son. What can I do for you?"

"New in town, ain't you?" The kid was a bright-eyed youngster about six years old.

"That's right. Just rode in."

The kid should have been able to see that for himself, if he wasn't blind. Which he obviously wasn't.

"You're dressed mighty fancy. You a gambler?"

Longarm didn't consider a brown tweed suit, vest, white shirt, and string tie all that fancy, but maybe it was for Warhorse. He relaxed in the saddle and thumbed back his flat-crowned, snuff-brown Stetson.

"No, I enjoy a game of cards as much as the next fella, but that ain't my line."

"What are you, then?"

Until Longarm located Ed Galloway, he didn't want to go blabbing to all and sundry that he packed a badge for Uncle Sam. You never could tell when even a despicable skunk like Galloway might have made a few friends in a place. So Longarm grinned at the kid.

"A fella who minds his own business, that's what I am."

"Oh." The answer didn't seem to bother the youngster. "You wouldn't be lookin' for a girl, would you?"

Longarm frowned. If this kid was out trying to pimp his big sis to strangers, Longarm would be sorely tempted to climb down from the horse and paddle his butt.

"What do you mean by that?"

"Well, you look like a sturdy enough fella, and my mama's lookin' for a new husband so I'll have a pa again—"

"Jasper McKittredge! Where in the world have you gotten off to?"

The woman's voice made Longarm look around. She was coming from a building on the other side of the street. Words painted on the front window read WARHORSE TRIBUNE. Looked like even a little place like this had a newspaper.

The woman came up to Longarm's horse. "Is my son bothering you, sir?"

"No, he was just, uh, welcoming me to town, I reckon you might say."

The kid came around in front of Longarm's horse with the mutt trailing him.

"I thought this fella might be interested in marryin' up with you, Ma. He's new in town, so he don't know yet that you got a bad temper."

The woman looked like she was fixing to cloud up and rain all over the boy, sort of like the sky above Warhorse. It didn't make her any less pretty, though, Longarm noted. She pointed to the newspaper office.

"You march right back in there and finish sweeping up, Jasper, unless you want me to tan your behind."

The kid didn't look all that scared. "All right, Ma." He started toward the office, snapping his fingers to get the dog to follow him. Then he paused to wave at Longarm. "So long, mister. You think about it. I could use a new pa."

The woman sighed and shook her head as the boy went on inside the building. She looked up at Longarm and pushed some of the thick mahogany hair that framed her face back over her right ear.

"I'm sorry about that, Mister . . . ?"

"Long." Longarm tugged politely on the brim of his hat. "Custis Long."

"I'm Adele McKittredge. Della, the people around here call me."

"Pleased to make your acquaintance, Mrs. McKittredge." Longarm had seen the wedding ring on her finger and assumed she was a widow, based on what her son Jasper had said about needing a new father.

Any man who married Della McKittredge would be getting a pretty wife, that was for sure. She was a little on the short side but had a well-curved body in a simple gray wool dress. Her eyes were a deep, rich brown, almost as dark as the thick waves of hair on her head. According to Jasper, she had a temper, but she also had a sweet smile.

Longarm wasn't in the market for a wife, though, no matter how pretty Della might be. Some of the deputy United States marshals who worked for Chief Marshal Billy Vail out of the Denver office were married, but Longarm had always thought it was a mite unfair for a man in such a dangerous profession to get hitched. A woman married to a frontier lawman stood a good chance of winding up a widow.

Of course, Della McKittredge had already lost one husband. From the looks of it, though, he hadn't been a star packer. Longarm nodded toward the office.

"Is that your newspaper, ma'am?"

"It is. I've been trying to keep it going since my husband passed away." She smiled. "With Jasper's help, of course."

"Must not be easy."

She shook her head. "No. It's not."

A thought occurred to Longarm. "Maybe you can help me. Since you run the newspaper, you must know most of the folks in town."

"I suppose. Are you looking for someone?"

"Hombre name of Ed Galloway."

Della frowned in thought for a moment. "I'm afraid that name's not familiar to me. Sorry."

Longarm wasn't particularly surprised. It would have been a long shot if the woman had known Galloway. An outlaw on the run like that would lie low. More than likely Galloway was holed up in some saloon or whore's crib . . . if he was even still here in Warhorse. Somebody had notified the authorities in Phoenix that they'd seen Galloway here, and the sheriff there had wired Billy Vail in Denver right away. This was the first lead to Galloway they had gotten in the two years since the train robbery, so Vail had ordered Longarm to rattle his hocks over to Warhorse. But despite hurrying, it had taken him three days to get here. Galloway could be long gone by now.

"Don't worry about it, ma'am. I'll find him."

"That sounds . . . ominous. Is there going to be trouble, Mr. Long?"

"I hope not."

"So do I. Warhorse, despite its name, is a peaceful town most of the time. Marshal Ryan sees to that. Maybe you should go talk to him about this man you're looking for."

Longarm tugged on the brim of his hat again. "That's exactly what I plan on doing, Mrs. McKittredge. Good day to you. And I'm sorry to disappoint your boy about that whole marrying business."

She laughed. "He'll get over it."

Longarm lifted his horse's reins and turned the mount to start up Warhorse's main street again. He intended to find the marshal's office and check in with the local badge toter.

Unfortunately, at that moment a couple of men ran out of one of the saloons not far in front of him and started shooting at him. Longarm heard the slugs whistling past him.

And behind him, Della McKittredge suddenly cried out in pain.

Chapter 2

Longarm realized a second later that the men weren't actually shooting *at* him. They were blazing away at each other instead, but they were firing so wildly that bullets were flying all around the street. It didn't matter who the intended targets were. A stray bullet could kill somebody just as dead as a perfectly aimed one.

So he allowed his instincts to take over in order to stop the carnage before it got any worse. His right hand flashed across his body to the cross-draw rig on his left hip and palmed out the Colt double-action Frontier revolver. The .44 roared and bucked against his palm as soon as he brought it around in line with the two yahoos who seemed to be intent on killing each other.

Longarm's first shot creased the forearm of one of the combatants. The man howled in pain and dropped his gun. The second slug from Longarm's Colt kicked up dust between the feet of the other man, making him hop frantically in the air and forget all about the man he'd been shooting at. He was more worried about keeping his toes from getting shot off.

"Drop it, old son!" Longarm's voice rang out clear and

strong in the street as the echoes of the gunplay died away. "Or the next round'll drop you!"

The second man's hand opened. His iron thudded to the dust in the street. He backed off, showing both open hands.

"Don't shoot, mister!"

Most of the folks who had been on the street had scurried for cover as soon as the shooting started. Now one man emerged from a building in the next block and ran toward the scene of the violence with a shotgun clutched in his hands. As he skidded to a halt a few yards away, he threw the Greener to his shoulder and leveled the barrels at Longarm.

"Drop that gun, mister!"

Longarm was annoyed about having the scattergun pointed at him. He had never cottoned to staring down the barrels of a Greener like that.

But he spotted the tin star pinned to the man's shirt and supposed he couldn't blame the local lawman for reacting like that. After all, the marshal of Warhorse didn't know him from Adam's off ox. The fella had heard all hell breaking loose in the streets of his town and had run out to see what was going on. Naturally, he was going to throw down on the one man still holding a gun and looking like he knew how to use it.

"Take it easy, Marshal." Longarm kept his voice steady and calm. He didn't drop his Colt, but he took his finger out of the trigger guard and held up both hands to show that he didn't intend to fire again. "Those two are the ones who were causing the ruckus. But I reckon what you'd better do first is check on Mrs. McKittredge. I think she was hit when all that lead started to fly."

Della stepped up alongside Longarm's horse. When he caught sight of her from the corner of his eye and turned to look at her, he saw that she had her left hand pressed to that side of her neck. He didn't notice any blood flowing from under her fingers, which was a relief.

"I'm all right." She lowered her hand, revealing a red mark on the side of her neck that looked like a burn. "I think one of the bullets grazed me . . ."

Then as her voice trailed away, her eyes rolled up in their sockets and her knees buckled. She fell in a limp heap.

Longarm was out of the saddle in a flash, pouching his iron as soon as his boots hit the ground. He dropped to a knee beside Della as the marshal hurried forward.

"What's wrong with her? Was she hit somewhere else?"

Longarm looked quickly over Della's body but didn't see any bloodstains on the dress.

"She don't appear to be hurt except for that bullet burn on her neck. My guess is that she realized just how close she came to dying and fainted."

Della's breasts rose and fell steadily, which was a good sign. Longarm unfastened the top button of her dress, which had been buttoned all the way up to her neck. She could breathe a little easier that way.

"Hold it, you two!"

Longarm glanced around and saw that the marshal was covering the two would-be gunslingers again with the shotgun.

"You're not going anywhere except jail!"

"But, Marshal, I'm hurt!" That whining complaint came from the man Longarm had winged. "I need the sawbones to look at this arm of mine."

"You're lucky I don't let you stand there and bleed to death. I'll fetch the doc, but he'll have to examine you in your jail cell, because you and Dennehy are going behind bars!"

The citizens of Warhorse were starting to gather now that the shooting was over. A couple of women stepped forward and offered to take care of Della McKittredge. Before they could do anything, though, her son Jasper sprinted up, with the yellow mutt bounding along behind him.

"Ma! Ma!"

Longarm caught hold of the frantic boy's shoulders. "Take it easy, son. Your ma's all right. She just fainted."

Jasper looked up at Longarm with wide, frightened eyes. "Fainted! Ma *never* faints! She didn't even faint when that runaway wagon team ran over Pa!"

So that's what had happened to the late Mr. McKittredge. Such deaths were tragic but not all that uncommon out here in the West, Longarm knew. The frontier had lots of different ways to kill a man.

Della let out a moan as her eyelids began to flicker. Longarm patted Jasper on the shoulder as the women helped her to her feet.

"See, she's gonna be all right. These ladies are gonna help her back over to the newspaper office. You run along with them, now."

Still sniffling, Jasper followed in the wake of the townswomen who were assisting his mother. Della was unsteady on her feet but didn't look like she was going to pass out again. Longarm watched them for a second, then turned back to the marshal.

The lawman was still covering the two gunmen with the Greener. He jerked his head toward the building he had come from in the next block.

"Come on down to the marshal's office with me, mister. I want to talk to you."

That was agreeable to Longarm. He'd been on his way to find the lawman when those two dime-novel desperadoes had started burning powder.

Longarm took up the reins of his horse to lead the animal. He and Marshal Ryan fell in step beside each other as Ryan herded his prisoners toward the jail. The one who'd been shot was still complaining bitterly. Blood that had run down his wounded arm dripped from his fingers. The large crimson droplets thudded into the dust.

Before the four men reached the marshal's office, equally large drops of rain began to fall, spaced out at first but then coming quicker and closer together. Thunder boomed and lightning flashed, causing Ryan to glance toward the threatening sky.

"Here it comes. Move, you two! Let's get inside before it really starts to rain!"

They didn't make it. A downpour began to sluice from the heavens. Everybody who was still out in the open dashed for cover, including Longarm, Marshal Ryan, and the two prisoners. The sky grew even darker and more ominous, as if night had come early to the town of Warhorse.

Rainwater ran in a steady stream off the brim of Longarm's hat by the time they reached the covered porch in front of the marshal's office. Longarm quickly looped the horse's reins around the hitch rail, then grabbed his Winchester, bedroll, and saddlebags. Carrying the gear, he followed Ryan and the prisoners out of the deluge and into the office.

Ryan already had the two gunmen in the cell block, which consisted of two cells facing each other across a narrow hallway at the rear of the office. The iron-barred doors clanged shut as he slammed them.

"Marshal, don't forget about fetchin' the doc for this arm of mine!"

Ryan shook his head. "When the rain lets up."

"But I might bleed to death by then! It really hurts, too."

Ryan sighed and turned to look at Longarm, who was leaning the Winchester in a corner of the office. "You know anything about patching up gunshot wounds?"

Longarm shrugged as he put his damp bedroll and saddlebags on the floor. "A little."

"All right. You plugged this asshole, you come patch him. Unless you'd rather go back out in that to find the doctor."

Longarm glanced out the door, which he had left open when he came in because his hands were full. The rain was coming down straight and hard in the street. Lightning flashed, and the tater wagon rolled over in heaven again. Longarm took off his hat and shook water from it.

"Reckon I'll pass."

Ryan raised his eyebrows and gestured toward the cell where the wounded man waited.

"Oh, hell. All right. Got any bandages?"

"Yep." Ryan came out of the cell block and went over to his desk. He set the Greener down, took a roll of bandages and a bottle of whiskey from one of the drawers, and held them out toward Longarm. "I keep the whiskey here strictly for medicinal purposes, of course."

"Of course."

Longarm took the bandages and bottle and went into the cell block. Out in the office, Ryan started rattling around the black, cast-iron stove in the corner.

"I'll get some coffee boiling."

"Sounds good." Longarm faced the wounded man. "Stick your arm out through the bars."

The man did so. Longarm took a barlow knife from his pocket and used it to cut away the blood-soaked sleeve, ignoring the man's complaint that he was ruining the shirt. Once he had the wound uncovered, he saw that his bullet had plowed a shallow furrow across the top of the man's forearm, knocking out a chunk of meat but missing the bone. It was a bloody, painful, but minor injury as long as it didn't fester.

Longarm guarded against that by dousing the wound liberally with raw whiskey. The prisoner yelped and cursed. Longarm grunted.

"If you're looking for sympathy, old son, you've come to the wrong place."

He cut a strip from the roll of bandages and made a pad out of it, then poured more whiskey on it and placed it over the wound. He wrapped the bandages around the man's arm to hold the pad in place, and when he had the wound bound up good and tight, he cut the strip of cloth and tied it off.

"That'll hold you until the rain stops and a real saw-bones can take a look at it. Just sit down on the bunk and hold your other arm under it to support it."

The man was pale, and a couple of tears had run down his cheeks from the pain. "I'm much obliged, I reckon . . . or at least I would be if you weren't the son of a bitch who shot me in the first place!"

Longarm suppressed the urge to growl at the hombre. The aroma of boiling coffee coming from the pot on the stove drew him out of the cellblock and back into the marshal's office. He had the roll of bandages in one hand and the whiskey bottle in the other.

That's why all he could do was stop and stare over the barrel of a six-shooter as Marshal Ryan pointed the weapon at him.

"All right, gunslinger . . . Who are you, and what the hell are you doing in my town?"

Chapter 3

Longarm didn't make any sudden moves. Ryan was a tall, rawboned man with a shock of red hair and a hard cast to his face. He might be just a small-town lawman, but he looked like he knew how to handle the revolver in his hand.

"Careful with that smokepole, Marshal. I'm not a gunslinger. If you'll let me put these things down, I can explain who I am."

Ryan jerked the barrel of the gun toward the desk. "Make the explanation fast, and it better be a good one."

Still moving cautiously, Longarm placed the bandages and whiskey on the desk, then stepped away from it. "I'm a deputy United States marshal. I'm gonna reach inside my coat, so I can show you my badge and bona fides."

Ryan's eyes widened slightly at the claim that the man in his office was a federal lawman. But after a moment, he nodded.

"All right. Just don't try any tricks."

"Wouldn't think of it."

Longarm slid his hand inside his coat. In doing so, his fingers brushed over the lump in the vest pocket on the other side from where he kept his watch. A gold chain ran from pocket to pocket, looping across his chest. The watch was attached to one end of it.

A .41-caliber, two-shot derringer was welded to the other end of the chain. The hideout gun had saved Longarm's bacon on many occasions in the past. He wasn't interested in shooting it out with Marshal Ryan, though, so he reached past the derringer to the inside pocket of his coat where he kept the leather folder that contained his badge and identification papers.

Longarm took out the folder, set it on the desk, and then backed off, still keeping his hands in sight at all times. "Take a look at that. You'll see that I'm telling the truth."

Ryan stepped forward. The Colt stayed rock steady in his hand as he picked up the folder with his other hand and flipped it open. His eyes flicked to the badge, and he grunted in surprise.

"Looks real."

"It is. Name's Custis Long. I work for Marshal Billy Vail, out of the Denver office."

A frown creased Ryan's forehead. "I think I've heard of you. You're the one they call Longarm, right?"

"Some do."

"Yeah, you look like the descriptions I've heard, come to think of it. I remember hearing about that mustache, and they say you look like you're part Indian."

Longarm shrugged. "Pure, hundred percent West by-God Virginian."

Ryan snapped the folder closed and tossed it back to Longarm, who caught it deftly and slipped it back into his pocket. The local lawman holstered his gun.

"Sorry, Marshal. All I knew about you was that you rode into Warhorse and did some mighty slick gun handling. Nobody would ever mistake either Coolidge and Dennehy for John Wesley Hardin, but they're not babes in the woods, either."

Longarm jerked a thumb at the cell block. "That'd be the two hombres you got cooling their heels in there?"

"That's right. Dex Coolidge and Mal Dennehy. Coolidge is the one you wounded. They've been around these parts for about a year. They do a little prospecting, sometimes ride grub line for one of the spreads to the east, but mostly they get drunk, argue, and try to kill each other. Until now it's always been fists, though. This is the first time they've gone to spraying lead around like that." A faint smile curved Ryan's lips. "Please tell me that you've come here to arrest one or both of them and get them out of my hair."

Longarm chuckled and shook his head. "Sorry, Marshal. I'm afraid I never heard of either of 'em. I *am* here looking for an owlhoot, though." He reached inside his coat again and this time took out a folded piece of paper. When he unfolded it and spread it on the corner of the desk, it was revealed to be a reward poster. "You ever hear of Ed Galloway?"

Ryan looked surprised again. "The train robber?"

"That's right."

"You think he's here in Warhorse?"

"Somebody claims to have spotted him here less than a week ago. They told the law in Phoenix, who passed the word on to us in Denver. I got here as fast as I could."

"Who said they saw Galloway here?" Ryan sounded skeptical about the idea the outlaw could be in Warhorse.

"Now, that I don't know. The information got lost somewhere along the way, if the fella ever gave his name to the authorities in Phoenix at all."

"So on the word of one man—a man whose identity you don't even know—you come all the way out here to Arizona Territory?"

Longarm's voice hardened. "We ain't seen hide nor hair of Galloway for two years, ever since him and his gang held up the *Colorado Flyer* and gunned down the conductor. He stole a bunch of U.S. government gold that day, and Uncle

Sam still wants him for it. *I* want him for killing Cullen Johnson."

"That'd be the conductor?"

"Yeah. Good friend of mine."

Ryan nodded. "Well, I reckon I don't blame you, then. I'd want to get that bastard Galloway in my sights, too."

"Oh, I won't kill him." Longarm shook his head. "Not unless he forces me to. I want to take him back so he can stand trial for what he did."

"Let the courts handle him, eh? Well, that's the proper thing to do, I suppose." Ryan started toward the stove as thunder rumbled again outside. The rain continued to pour down. "You want some coffee?"

"That'd be good. First, though . . . do you know if Galloway is here in Warhorse?"

Ryan shook his head. "Marshal, I don't even know what the son of a bitch looks like."

Longarm tapped the paper on the corner of the desk. "There's no picture of him on this reward dodger, but it's got a description of him. He stands six foot two and weighs about a hundred and sixty pounds."

"Sort of a scrawny fella, sounds like."

"Yeah. He's got long brown hair and a beard, and bushy eyebrows. They say he looks sort of like a preacher, but if he was, he'd be the snake-handling kind."

Ryan used a piece of leather to protect his hand as he picked up the coffeepot and poured the steaming black liquid into a couple of tin cups. "Sort of loco, in other words."

"Yeah. Seen anybody who looks like that around town in the past week?"

Ryan handed one of the cups to Longarm. "I'm sorry, Marshal, but I sure haven't, and I keep a pretty close eye on who's in town and who isn't." He hesitated. "You know, though, that this fella could have changed his appearance. Sometimes a man will do that when he's on the run from the law."

"I suppose so. But I don't have anything else to go by except that description."

Ryan sipped his coffee. "Tell you what I'll do. I'll ask around town and see what I can find out." He sat down behind the desk. "You know, it might be a wise idea if you kept quiet about who you really are and let me do some poking around first. If this fella Galloway really *is* here and finds out that a federal lawman is in town looking for him, he's liable to get spooked and take off for the tall and uncut."

Longarm propped a hip on the front corner of the desk. "I sort of had the same thing in mind." He frowned as a thought occurred to him. "Might be a problem, though. Before all that ruckus started, while I was talking to Mrs. McKittredge, I asked her about Galloway and used his name."

"Della McKittredge may run the newspaper, but she's not the type to go gabbing all over town about anything. We just need to talk to her and ask her to be discreet."

"She'd do that?"

Ryan nodded. "I think so."

"If she's like every other newspaper editor I ever ran into, she'll want something in return . . . like a promise that we'll let her in on what's going on, even though she can't print it yet."

The local lawman took another sip of coffee and thought about that for a moment before nodding again. "You're probably right. I think she's trustworthy, though."

Longarm heard a note of admiration in Ryan's voice and wondered if the man had taken a shine to the widow after the late Mr. McKittredge got himself run down by that wagon. It was possible . . . but it was also none of his business. He inclined his head toward the office door, which was still open to let in some air. The day was warm, despite the rain.

"We can go talk to her if that rain ever lets up."

"I'm not sure it's going to." Ryan stood up and walked over to peer out at the street. Lightning flashed again, lighting up his rawboned face for a second. "It looks like it's liable to rain the rest of the day and all night. You got a slicker?"

"Rolled up in my blankets."

"Maybe we'd better go see her now, just in case. The quieter we keep this, the better."

Longarm wasn't sure that was necessary, but on the other hand, he didn't want word of his mission leaking out and getting to Galloway if the train robber really was here. He downed the rest of the hot, bitter coffee and then set the empty cup on the desk.

"That's fine with me. Also, I'd sort of like to make sure the lady's all right."

Ryan reached for his hat, which hung on a nail beside a rack that held several rifles and shotguns. "I was thinking the same thing. My slicker's in the back room where my cot is. Don't have much use for rain gear around here. It's dry nearly all the time."

The lawman went through a narrow door into his sleeping quarters. It couldn't be much of a life he led, living and working in this small, dingy building, Longarm thought. But that was the lot of a small-town peace officer. Many of them never married, drifting from place to place, job to job, never settling down, until one day they were just a mite too careless and some drunken cowboy got off a lucky shot and blew a hole in them.

Not that Longarm's life was all that much better, he reminded himself as he thought about his rented room back in Denver. But at least he got to travel a lot and had seen just about all there was to see west of the Mississippi, and all the way down into Mexico and up to Canada, too. Anyway, he'd been a lawman for so long that it was the only life he knew anymore.

He took his yellow oilcloth slicker from his bedroll while Ryan was in the back room. When both men were protected as much as they could be from the rain, they tugged their hats down tightly and stepped out into the downpour. The rain pounded at them as thunder boomed again.

In the flash of lightning that accompanied the thunder, Longarm suddenly saw half a dozen riders trotting up the street toward him and Ryan. In that split-second glimpse through the rain, the men on their tall horses looked like some sort of otherworldly creatures, vague and threatening. As the flash disappeared, so did the strangers on horseback.

Ryan must have seen them, too, because he came to an abrupt halt and stared in that direction. Lightning flashed again, and Longarm saw that the men had angled their mounts over to one of the saloons. They were dismounting in front of the place now, swinging down from their saddles and looping their reins around the hitch rail. They were probably just cowhands from one of the spreads in the area, Longarm thought, although it was a little unusual for punchers to be coming to town in weather like this.

It probably hadn't been raining when they started to the settlement, though, and Longarm had done enough cowboying himself to know such men wouldn't let a little threatening weather keep them from a chance to get drunk, gamble, and bed down with a whore. He looked over at Ryan, who was still standing there.

"Something wrong, Marshal?"

Ryan shook his head. "No, I was just watching to see where those fellas went. I like to keep track of things like that."

"You recognize them?"

"With all this rain, I didn't get a good look at them." Ryan started walking along the street again. "Come on, let's pay that visit to Mrs. McKittredge, and then I guess I'd better see about getting the doc to look at Coolidge's arm."

Longarm fell in step beside Ryan again as they slogged up the muddy street. He didn't have any reason to disbelieve what the local lawman had just told him.

But he had a hunch Ryan hadn't told him everything he knew about those six riders, either.

Chapter 4

The two lawmen stomped their feet on the porch in front of the newspaper office to get some of the mud off their boots. The gunmetal sky had darkened to the color of charcoal. A lamp burned inside the office, casting a yellow glow through the window.

Della McKittredge must have heard the racket Longarm and Ryan were making, because she jerked the door open to peer out at them with wide eyes.

"Oh! Hello, Pat. I knew somebody was out here, but I didn't expect it to be you and Mr. Long."

Pat Ryan tugged on the brim of his hat and nodded politely to her. "Hello, Della. We just wanted to see how you're doing after that incident in the street a while ago."

"I'm fine." She gestured toward a small bandage on her neck. "Dr. Chamberlain came by and put some medicine on that little bullet burn. He said it was nothing to worry about."

"That's good to know."

She gave an awkward laugh. "I'm just embarrassed because I fainted like that and scared everybody."

"No reason to be embarrassed. You wouldn't be normal if you weren't upset in a situation like that."

Della stepped back. "Why don't the two of you come in?"

"We're liable to drip water on your floor . . ."

"Oh, goodness, you don't think I'm worried about a little water, do you?" She motioned them through the door. "Come in, come in."

Longarm and Ryan entered the office. The homey smell of food cooking came through a door that opened into the rear of the building. Della and Jasper evidently had their living quarters back there. Longarm wondered if anybody in this town had a house that was separate from their business.

"I had just started fixing supper. I can make the stew bigger if the two of you would like to stay."

Ryan shook his head. "No, we're much obliged, but we couldn't impose."

"It wouldn't be an imposition."

"I, uh, promised Mr. Long here that I'd show him around town."

Della frowned. "In this rain? It's not very good weather for sightseeing. Not that there are many sights worth seeing in Warhorse."

"Well, I, uh . . ." Ryan rubbed at his jaw in awkward discomfort. "Is the doc still here?"

"No, he said he was going back to his house in case anybody came looking for him. Do you need him?"

"Got to get him to take a look at Dex Coolidge's arm."

"Oh, that's right. He was wounded worse than I was. How is he?"

"Don't waste any sympathy on a troublemaking hard case like him, ma'am." The words came out of Ryan's mouth sharper than Longarm figured the marshal intended. Ryan confirmed that with a grimace. "Sorry, Della. Didn't mean to sound like that. But you don't have to worry about Coolidge. He'll be fine. I want the doc to look at him just to shut up his bellyaching, as much as anything."

Della smiled. "All right, then. To tell the truth, I wasn't

really all that worried about him to start with. He and that Dennehy have done nothing but cause trouble ever since they came to Warhorse."

"That's the truth." Ryan lowered his voice. "There's something else we'd like to discuss with you, if you've got a minute. Where's Jasper?"

A confused frown creased Della's forehead. "He's on the back porch, playing with that stray dog he's taken in. I told him to stay out of the rain, but a boy and a dog . . . well, let's just say that I won't be surprised if he's muddy when he comes in." She looked back and forth between Longarm and Ryan. "Is this something you don't want him to hear?"

Ryan nodded. "If it's all right with you, we'd just as soon that it stays between the three of us, at least for now."

"You haven't forgotten that you're talking to a newspaper editor, have you, Pat?"

"I'm asking as a personal favor . . ."

"Of course." She nodded quickly. "I'm sorry. I haven't forgotten how kind you've been to me." Her eyes moved over to Longarm. "You're a lawman, too, aren't you?"

"Yes, ma'am. Deputy U.S. marshal."

"Yes, now that I know, I can tell by looking at you. The two of you are cut from the same cloth. Is your name really Custis Long?"

Longarm grinned. "That much was sure enough true."

"And you're looking for someone. That man Ed Galloway you mentioned." Della's frown deepened. "I keep thinking I've heard that name before, but I'm certain he's not anyone who lives around here."

"Well, he's probably not using that name, since he's a fugitive on the run from the law."

Her eyes widened. "Oh! I remember now. That train robbery a few years ago. Ed Galloway was the leader of the gang that stopped the *Colorado Flyer*!"

"Yes, ma'am. And he gunned down a friend of mine who

was working as the conductor on that train, too. The law's been looking for him ever since—"

"And you think he's hiding out here in Warhorse!" Della was suddenly breathless with excitement.

Longarm nodded. "We got word that he might be."

Ryan spoke up again. "Marshal Long and I have talked it over, and we agree that it'd be a good idea if folks here in town didn't find out who he is just yet. I'm going to see what I can find out about this fella Galloway."

"He'd have to be someone who came to town in the past two years. That's how long it's been since that holdup, isn't it?"

Longarm tugged at his right earlobe and then ran his thumbnail along the line of his jaw as he frowned in thought. "You're probably right, but we don't know much about Galloway. It's possible he could've been in Warhorse longer than that. He might have been using this place as a hideout between jobs."

Ryan shook his head. "There's nobody who fits the description you gave me in town. We already talked about that."

"Well, you can only eat an apple one bite at a time. You can ask around, like you said, and if that don't turn up anything, we'll hash it out more then."

"Fine." Ryan turned his attention back to Della. "I reckon we can count on you to keep all this to yourself for the time being?"

"For the time being." She folded her arms across her chest and looked at Longarm. "But if you find this outlaw and arrest him, Marshal Long, I'll expect you to sit down for an interview with me so I can get the whole story. Something like this might even get picked up by the newspapers in Phoenix and Tucson."

Longarm smiled. "I reckon I could do that. Talking to newspaper folks ain't one of my favorite things to do . . . but I don't think I ever had one as pretty as you asking me questions, ma'am."

Della blushed. "Don't think flattery will make me any less determined to get the story."

"Not for a second, ma'am."

With the deal struck, Della turned her attention back to more domestic matters. "You're sure you won't stay for supper?"

Ryan shook his head. "No, I reckon I'd better go ahead and fetch Doc Chamberlain for that wounded prisoner."

"It's still pouring out there."

"Have to go out in it sometime."

Della crossed her arms again. A shiver ran through her as lightning flashed and thunder rumbled.

"I don't like storms like this. We get them so seldom around here, I guess I never really get used to them. When it gets so dark and ominous like this, I . . . I feel like something terrible is going to happen."

Longarm knew what she meant. He had gradually come to realize that an air of tension gripped Warhorse. He could see it in the stiff way Marshal Pat Ryan stood. And the brooding heaviness of the air earlier, before the storm broke, could have contributed to the outbreak of violence between Dex Coolidge and Mal Dennehy. Sometimes when a man's nerves are stretched taut, he's quicker to take offense, more eager to grab for a gun at the slightest excuse.

Longarm and Ryan both tugged their hat brims and then stepped out of the newspaper office. There was only a narrow awning over the porch here, so the hard rain pelted them almost immediately.

Ryan pointed up the street and raised his voice to be heard over the rain and the almost constant rumbling of thunder. "The doctor's office is up this way!"

He led off with long-legged strides. Longarm was slightly taller than the local lawman, so he didn't have any trouble keeping up. The slicker he wore was a good one and kept him fairly dry, but somehow a little trickle of rain found its way to his neck and wormed its way under his collar and down his back. That always happened. Longarm figured it was a law of the universe or some such.

After a couple of blocks, Ryan turned in, opening a gate in a picket fence that ran around a small yard in front of a neat house. "This is where Doc Chamberlain lives. His practice is in front, and he lives in the back."

"Of course he does."

"What?"

Longarm shook his head. "Never mind. He may not take kindly to you asking him to come out in this weather."

"He's a doctor. He ought to be used to being inconvenienced by now. Sort of like a lawman."

That was true enough. Longarm followed Ryan up a flagstone walk to the porch. The sawbones was a little slow in answering Ryan's knock, but after a minute or two the door swung open.

"Howdy, Doc."

The physician sighed. "I've been expecting you, Marshal, ever since I heard that one of the men you arrested was wounded. Let me get my coat and my bag." Chamberlain paused. "Who's that with you?"

"Oh, this is, uh, Custis Long."

Chamberlain was a tall, thin-faced man with silvery hair, dark pouches under his eyes, and prominent eyebrows that now lifted in surprise. "The man who was involved in the shooting?"

"That's right. He patched up Dex Coolidge's arm, temporary-like."

Chamberlain looked at Longarm. "You have medical training, Mr. Long?"

Longarm shook his head. "No, but I've lived long enough to see a few bullet wounds in my time. I just cleaned the crease in that hombre's arm with whiskey and bandaged it up."

"From the sound of it, you did what needed to be done,

but I'll take a look and make sure. I'll be right with you, gentlemen."

Chamberlain went back into the house, and while they waited for him to reappear, Ryan turned to Longarm. "You reckon you could take the doc back to the jail?"

"I suppose so, but where are you gonna be?"

The lawman made a vague gesture up and down the street. "I need to make my evening rounds. It's usually a little later when I do that, but with this storm, night's falling early today."

"You plan on making your rounds even in this rain?"

"The responsibilities of the job don't go away when the weather's bad." Ryan lowered his voice. "I expect you know that."

Longarm shrugged. It was true that he had pursued fugitives in all sorts of weather, from howling blizzards to choking sandstorms. He had waited patiently to get the drop on some owlhoot when it was twenty below zero and when it was a hundred and ten in the shade. The law didn't care whether the men who enforced it were comfortable.

"Yeah, I know what you mean. Don't worry, I'll see to it that the doc gets to the jail safe and sound."

"I'm not expecting any trouble, you understand. Just being careful."

"Sure." Longarm lifted a hand in farewell as Ryan walked off into the rain.

Chamberlain emerged from the house a moment later wearing a black slicker and a soft felt hat. He had his black medical bag in his hand.

"Where's Marshal Ryan?"

"He went to make his evening rounds."

Chamberlain shook his head. "That doesn't surprise me. I've never seen a lawman more devoted to his duties than Patrick Ryan."

They started toward the marshal's office and jail.

"Ryan been wearing the star here for long?"

"A couple of years, maybe more. I don't really know, Mr. Long. He was the marshal here when I arrived in Warhorse, not quite two years ago."

"You haven't been practicing here for very long, then?"

"No, I was in Prescott before that. But the doctor who was here before me, old Dr. Blaine, was friends with my father, and when he retired, he wrote and asked me if I'd be interested in taking over his practice. As a favor to him, I did . . . but I've found that I like it here most of the time. The dry climate agrees with me."

Longarm had to laugh. "The climate ain't too dry this evening!"

"Oh, but it will be again, once this storm blows over."

They reached the marshal's office and went inside. Complaining voices came from the cellblock.

"When's the doc gonna get here to look at my arm?" That was Coolidge.

"You're gonna have to give us some supper if you keep us locked up here!" The hungry one was Dennehy.

Longarm stepped into the corridor between the cells. "Hold your horses, both of you. The doc's here, Coolidge. I don't know anything about supper, but when Marshal Ryan gets back, I reckon he'll tend to it."

That wasn't good enough for Dennehy. "You could go over the café and get us something. Hell, you're the one responsible for us bein' in here."

"Yeah, the fact that the two of you are dumb enough to start slinging lead around the street didn't have anything to do with it." Longarm snorted in disgust. "You idiots came within a whisker of killing Mrs. McKittredge."

"Who?"

Dennehy answered his wounded cohort's question. "That pretty newspaper lady."

"Oh." Coolidge had the good grace to look at least a little crestfallen. "That would'a been a fuckin' shame. She's a fine-lookin' gal."

Dr. Chamberlain made an impatient gesture. "Stick your arm out here so I can take a look at that dressing. I may want to clean the wound again."

"Be careful, Doc. It already hurts like a son of a bitch."

Longarm started to step back out into the office, but Dennehy called a request after him. "If you go to the café to get our meals, see if you can get that waitress called Julia to bring 'em over. She's even prettier'n that newspaper lady."

Longarm was about to tell Dennehy that he had no intention of fetching any meals for them, and even less of asking some innocent waitress to do it, when he heard something that made his head jerk toward the open doorway.

Down the street, guns had begun to roar. Storm or no storm, hell was popping in Warhorse.

Chapter 5

Even though Chamberlain didn't know he was a lawman, Longarm turned to fling a command at the sawbones.

"Stay here and lock the door behind me! I'm gonna go see what all the ruckus is about."

He paused long enough as he hurried past the desk to lean over and blow out the lamp. It was getting dark enough outside now that a glow from inside might silhouette him in the doorway and make a better target of him.

Of course, whatever the trouble was, it wasn't his responsibility. It was Marshal Pat Ryan's job to keep the peace in Warhorse.

But no badge toter worth his salt would stand by and let hell break loose around him. That was why Longarm had taken cards in the shootout between Coolidge and Dennehy, and that was he charged out of the marshal's office now and turned toward the sound of gunfire.

Even through the rain and the gathering gloom, he saw muzzle flashes stab out on both sides of the street like they were trying to rival the lightning. On the near side, one man was crouched behind a parked buckboard. It didn't give him much cover, but there was nothing better close by. Across the street, Colt flame bloomed in several places.

As best Longarm could tell, the odds were at least four to one.

He didn't know who was involved, but he didn't like those odds. Anyway, he had a hunch the lone man behind the buckboard might be Marshal Pat Ryan.

Still, there was a chance he could be taking the wrong side, so as he drew his gun and ran through the rain, he fired high toward the men on the far side of the street. A couple crouched behind a water trough, and the other two were in the black mouth of an alley. Longarm triggered blue whistlers toward them, trying to put the shots close enough to spook the bushwhackers into running without actually hitting any of them.

He knew they were ones who had launched the ambush. One man wouldn't be fool enough to bushwhack four, no matter who he was.

He succeeded in drawing some of the fire away from the man behind the buckboard. Gun flame spurted at him. He dropped to a knee behind a rain barrel that was already overflowing with water. Bullets thudded into it but couldn't get through.

Longarm heard a swift rataplan of pounding hoofbeats over the rain. A group of horses splashed up the muddy street. He risked a look and in the glare from the lightning saw two men galloping along, leading several more mounts with empty saddles. They were trying to get to the gunmen on the far side of the street, he realized.

The shooting stopped abruptly. The men who'd been hiding behind the water trough lunged into the open and leaped into their saddles. The two from the alley followed right behind them. As soon as their butts hit leather, they dug in their spurs and sent the horses racing ahead.

The man at the buckboard stood up and threw a couple of shots after the fleeing bushwhackers, but the rain was so heavy it was already hard to see them in the shadows. Longarm didn't figure that either of those parting shots found its target unless it was by sheer luck.

He hustled toward the man by the buckboard, who turned sharply toward him.

"Don't shoot, old son! We're on the same side!"

"Long?" That was Ryan's voice, all right. "Is that you?"

Longarm came up to the local lawman. "Yeah. I was down at the jail with the doc and heard the shots. Figured I'd best see what was going on."

"You keep sticking your nose in every time there's trouble, folks are going to figure out that you're a lawman."

Longarm grunted. "You're welcome. Looked like those fellas had you pinned down pretty good, with no place to run and no good place to hide."

Ryan had started reloading his Colt, thumbing fresh cartridges into the empty chambers in the cylinder. "Yeah, you're right. They had me between a rock and a hard place. Thanks for lending a hand."

It was a grudging expression of gratitude, but better than nothing, Longarm supposed. "Why'd they jump you, anyway?"

"Damned if I know." Ryan snapped the Colt's cylinder closed. "I was just finishing up my rounds when they opened up on me. I was lucky to make it to that buckboard before I got ventilated."

"Lucky you didn't get ventilated after that." Longarm pulled his slicker back to get fresh bullets for his own gun from the loops on his shell belt. That let more rain in, but being wet beat being caught short on ammunition. Beat it all to hell and back. "I know one thing . . . I've got a hunch those hombres were the ones we saw riding in a while ago."

"The ones who went into Kilroy's saloon?" Ryan didn't sound convinced. "What makes you think that?"

"There were six of 'em. Unless I miscounted, there were four bushwhackers and two more fellas with the horses."

"That's not proof."

"No, but it's enough for my gut." Longarm finished re-loading his gun, leaving one chamber empty for the hammer to rest on. He slid the Colt back into leather. "I left the doc at the jail. You need him to take a look at you?"

"No, I wasn't hit. I'm fine. Just wet and mad."

Longarm knew the feeling.

The two men went back down the street to the marshal's office. Dr. Randall Chamberlain was waiting inside, sipping from a cup of coffee.

The doctor raised the cup in a sort of salute to Longarm and Ryan when they came in. "Hope you don't mind that I helped myself to the coffeepot, Pat."

"Not at all, Doc. How's the prisoner?"

"You mean Dex Coolidge?" Chamberlain nodded toward Longarm. "Mr. Long here did a good job of patching him up. An excellent job, in fact. I cleaned the wound with carbolic acid and rebandaged it, but I suspect Coolidge would have been just fine even if I hadn't. If you haven't had any medical training, Mr. Long, you must have had a lot of practical experience."

Longarm smiled and shrugged. "More than my share, maybe."

Chamberlain gestured toward the street. "What about that shooting that caused Mr. Long to hurry out of here? Is there anyone else I need to patch up?"

Ryan shook his head. "Not tonight. A bunch of cowboys took some potshots at me, but I wasn't hit and as far as I know, none of them were, either. I can't be sure of that because they rode out of town in a hurry."

"Why would they open fire on you like that?"

"You got me, Doc. Just blowing off steam, maybe. You know how loco those cowhands can get, especially when they've been swilling down that rotgut in Kilroy's."

"I suppose so." Chamberlain finished his coffee, set the empty cup down, and picked up his hat and medical bag.

He went over to the door, put on the hat, and shrugged into his slicker, which had been hanging on a nail beside the door, dripping water. "I'm going home. No need to accompany me."

"You sure, Doc?"

"My hope is that all the trouble is over for the night."

"Mine, too." Ryan's voice was as weary as the physician's.

The prisoners must have heard the men in the office talking. No sooner had Chamberlain gone out the door than they started complaining again.

"Hey, Marshal, if you're gonna keep us locked up in here, you got to feed us!"

"That's right, Marshal. We're hungry!"

Ryan grimaced. "They're right. They may be troublemakers, but it's the town's responsibility to feed prisoners. I guess I'd better go over to the café and see about getting something for them."

"How long do you plan to keep them locked up?"

"I'm charging them with disturbing the peace and attempted murder. Judge Hartley can hear the case tomorrow, I reckon. They'll just get a fine for disturbing the peace, but attempted murder is a more serious charge. They'll have to go to Phoenix for a trial in a state court, and then they're looking at a prison sentence of several years, at least." Ryan paused. "Or I can drop the attempted murder charges in return for the two of them riding out of here and never coming back."

Longarm chuckled. "That sounds like a good deal all the way around." He jerked a thumb toward the cellblock. "They said something earlier about a café. I'm a mite hungry myself, so I think I'll walk over there with you."

"All right. I'm going to lock the office door this time, so nobody can waltz in here and turn those prisoners loose. That's not likely to happen—those hombres don't have any real friends in Warhorse—but I'd just as soon not take the chance."

Ryan was a cautious man, not an uncommon quality in star packers. Longarm believed in not taking unnecessary chances, too. That was one reason he had lived as long as he had.

The two lawmen hadn't taken their slickers off. They left the marshal's office now, with Ryan locking the door behind them after he'd told Coolidge and Dennehy to settle down, that he was going to get them something to eat. Ryan angled across the muddy street toward a squarish stone building with a tile roof. Light glowed in all its windows. As they came closer, Longarm made out a sign on the awning above the boardwalk that ran in front of the building. It read RED TOP CAFÉ.

The place smelled mighty good, Longarm discovered as he and Ryan stepped inside, even better than the newspaper office where Della McKittredge had been cooking stew. There the aroma from the kitchen had been mixed with the sharp tang of printer's ink. Here there was only a tantalizing blend of spices, roasting meat, fresh-baked bread, and coffee.

A counter with stools in front of it ran along the right-hand wall. Round tables with blue-checked tablecloths took up the rest of the room. A swinging door behind the counter obviously led into the kitchen. A chalkboard on the wall gave the day's specials. The place was like countless other frontier cafés Longarm had seen. There was a comforting feel to it, and the enticing aromas made his stomach growl with hunger.

He felt a completely different sort of hunger as he saw the young woman who came out from behind the counter carrying a tray loaded down with platters of food.

Chapter 6

Long hair the color of pale honey framed the waitress's face and spilled over her shoulders. She wore a blue gingham dress with a square-cut neckline that was low enough to reveal the tops of the swelling mounds of her breasts.

When she glanced toward the two men who had just come in, Longarm saw that her eyes were a deep blue, a little darker than the dress she wore. She smiled at them, and even though Longarm knew the smile was probably directed at Marshal Ryan, it made an even stronger pang of desire go through him.

"You and your friend have a seat anywhere, Marshal. I'll be with you in a minute."

"Thanks, Julia." Ryan took off his hat, shook rainwater from it, and hung it on a hat tree.

Longarm did likewise and then hung his slicker on a coat rack just inside the door, where several other slickers were already hanging. The café wasn't packed, but it was doing a decent business with close to a dozen customers. The food had to be as good as it smelled, to get that many people to come out in a storm like this.

A thunderclap so loud that it made the floor shiver rolled over the café. Julia gasped and stumbled a little, and the tray in her hands started to tilt under the weight of the food. Longarm saw that happening and stepped forward quickly to reach out and grab it, steadying the tray so that Julia didn't drop it.

That brought another smile from her, this one strictly for him. "Thanks, mister. That was almost a big mess."

"Glad to oblige." Longarm let go of the tray when he was sure she had it under control again.

He and Ryan sat down at one of the empty tables. The local lawman smiled.

"That was quick action, Mr. Long."

"Call me Custis. I never could abide seeing good food go to waste, and it would have been a plumb waste if it had spilled all over the floor."

"I can't argue with that."

Julia came over to the table a minute later, after serving the food she'd brought out to several men at another table. "What can I get for you and your friend, Marshal?"

"Tell Arnie to fry us up some steaks with plenty of those German potatoes and the rest of the usual fixin's. And by the way, this fella is Custis Long. Custis, meet Julia Foster."

"The pleasure's mine, ma'am."

"Thank you, Mr. Long."

"By the way, Julia, you may have heard I have a couple of prisoners over in the jail, so I guess I'd better not let them starve. Tell Arnie to fix up some meals for them. I'll take the trays back over there once I've had my own supper."

"Charge the town for them, as usual?"

"That's right."

Julia nodded. "You want coffee?"

Both men said that they did. Julia smiled at them again, then went to deliver their order to Arnie, who was obviously the cook and probably the owner of this place, Longarm thought.

"Dennehy was saying earlier that he wanted Julia to bring them their meals. Now I know why."

Ryan grunted. "She's a mighty pretty girl, all right. Prettiest in town, maybe. Although there are some that would say . . . well, never mind."

"That the widow McKittredge is prettier?" Longarm grinned. "Speaking for myself, that's a choice I'd sure hate to have to make."

Ryan leaned forward slightly and clasped his hands together on the table. "Della's had a rough time of it. First losing her husband like that, then trying to raise the boy and keep the newspaper running by herself."

"Probably be a mite easier on her if she had another hombre who was interested in her . . . say, a fine, upstanding fella like the local marshal. That'd probably make little Jasper happy, too."

Ryan glared across the table. "I don't think a diaper and a bow and arrow suit you all that well. The woman lost her husband. I think she probably needs some time to get over that, don't you?"

"How long's it been since that wagon ran over her husband? Two years? Most folks would say that's long enough."

"Well, maybe I'm not most folks."

Julia came back to the table with cups, saucers, and a coffeepot. She filled the cups. "Your food will be ready in a few more minutes."

Longarm nodded his thanks and sipped the coffee. It was considerably better than what Ryan made in the jail.

"Is there a hotel in this town?"

"Not to speak of. There's a boardinghouse where some of the miners stay, and Kilroy will rent you a room on the second floor of his saloon." Ryan paused. "If you want one of the girls who works there to keep you company, that'll cost you extra."

Longarm shook his head. "That ain't what I'm looking

for tonight. Maybe the fella who owns the livery stable will let me bed down in his hayloft."

"Maybe so."

Julia brought out their food a few minutes later. The plates were heaped high with steaks, potatoes, greens, and biscuits. There were bowls of gravy and a pitcher of molasses. Longarm and Ryan dug in, and Longarm found to his pleasure that the meal tasted as good as it smelled.

He took his time eating, so that he could both savor the food and enjoy watching Julia move around the café. Finally, though, he had mopped up the last bit of gravy with the final bite of one of the fluffy biscuits and emptied his cup of the last drop of Arbuckles.

Ryan pushed his plate away and sighed. "After a meal like that, a man doesn't want to go back out in the rain. Reckon I've got to, though."

"I'll come down to your office tomorrow and see what you've found out about that other business."

"That'll be fine." Ryan pulled a watch out of his pocket and flipped it open. "You know, the café will be closing in another half hour or so. If you were to wait around, Julia might not mind if you were to walk her home."

"Now who's wearing a diaper and toting a bow and arrow?"

Ryan snapped the watch closed and lowered his voice. "A lot of nights, I keep an eye on her until she's home safe. She doesn't know about it, though, and I'd appreciate it if you wouldn't tell her. The fever got her folks a couple of years ago, not long after I came here. I guess the town sort of adopted her after that."

"She's a grown woman, you know. Must be twenty years old."

"Yeah, but . . . Just walk her home, blast it."

Longarm grinned. "I'd be glad to, as long as the lady agrees." He gestured toward the watch as Ryan started to put it away. "That's a mighty nice-looking timepiece. Trainman's watch, ain't it?"

Ryan held it out on the palm of his hand for a moment. "Yeah. My pa was an engineer for the Union Pacific. He passed it on to me before he died."

"It must keep good time, then."

"To the second." Ryan slid the watch into his pocket and stood up. "See you tomorrow, Custis."

He got his slicker and hat and left the café. Only a few customers remained now. Julia came out of the kitchen a minute later, looked around, and then walked over to the table.

"Can I get you anything else, Mr. Long?"

"Call me Custis. No, I'm fine. I just thought I might be bold enough to ask you if you'd allow me the honor of walking home after the café closes up."

The invitation evidently took her a little by surprise, but a smile broke across her face. "I'd like that." She paused. "Marshal Ryan didn't put you up to it, did he?"

"Why in the world would he do that?"

She leaned closer and her voice took on a conspiratorial tone. "He doesn't like for me to know that he's so protective of me. I've seen him keeping an eye on me lots of nights when I walk home."

Longarm managed not to laugh, but he couldn't stop the smile that tugged at his mouth. "Sort of a mother hen, is he?"

Julia shook her head. "Oh, it's not just me. He watches out for *everybody* in this town. I don't think I've ever seen a more devoted lawman than Pat Ryan. I'm not sure how he even finds time to sleep, he works so hard at his job."

"Well, that's just the sort of lawman every town needs, I reckon. Warhorse is lucky to have him."

"That's the truth. If you're going to be waiting for me, why don't I bring you another cup of coffee?"

"I'd be much obliged."

Longarm sipped on coffee to pass the time until the last customer left the café. A burly man with thinning hair and thick muttonchop whiskers came out of the kitchen. He wore an apron, and his shirtsleeves were rolled up over beefy forearms. He came around the counter and walked over to the table where Longarm sat.

"I'm Arnie Davidson." He stuck out a paw. "Julia tells me you're gonna walk her home."

Longarm stood up and shook hands with the proprietor. "Custis Long."

"You're a friend of the marshal's?"

"That's right." It was stretching the truth a mite to make that claim, thought Longarm, since he had only known Ryan for a few hours, but it was a fact that he felt an instinctive liking for the local lawman.

"Pat Ryan's the salt of the earth. If he vouches for you, I reckon you can be trusted."

"I'd like to think so."

Davidson had left the kitchen door propped open. He turned toward it. "Julia, you can go on home. I'll finish cleanin' up."

She came out of the kitchen wiping her hands on a cloth. "Are you sure, Arnie?"

"You bet."

Julia smiled. "All right, thanks." She started toward the front door.

Longarm moved to intercept her. "Wait just a minute. Don't you have a slicker?"

She shook her head. "It wasn't raining when I came to work. I'll be all right. It's just water."

"You better take another look." Longarm plucked his slicker from the rack. It had dried while he and Ryan were eating. "It's a toad strangler out there. I want you to wear mine."

"But then you'll get soaked!"

"Don't worry about me. I did some cowboying in my younger days and rode many a night herd in the rain. It don't bother me none."

"Well . . . if you're sure . . ."

Longarm held the slicker so that she could slide her arms into the sleeves. Then he unbuttoned the hood and rolled it out so that she could pull it over her head. He normally kept it rolled up around the collar since he nearly always had his hat on whenever it was raining.

"This is awfully nice of you." They stepped out onto the boardwalk. "We'll hurry, so you won't have to get any wetter than you have to."

Longarm cupped his left hand under her right elbow, and with that they set off down the street, moving at a trot through the downpour.

Chapter 7

Julia lived in a small, neat frame house on one of the side streets, just around the corner from a general store that was closed for the night even though it would normally still be open at this time. The rain had driven almost everybody indoors by now, and some businesses were closing early.

She laughed as she and Longarm dashed up onto the porch. "See, I told you that you'd get soaked!"

Longarm grinned as he tried to shake water off himself without much success. "Looks like you were right. I'll bet Warhorse has gotten more rain since this storm started this afternoon than it gets in a month most of the time."

"A month? I'm not sure we get this much rain in a year!" She opened the front door. "Come inside."

"I don't know that I ought to—"

"For goodness' sake! I won't tell Marshal Ryan if you don't, and in weather like this, I doubt if anyone is spying on us. You can at least hang up your coat and let it dry for a little while. You'll have your slicker when you go back out."

"Well, I reckon that's true." Longarm followed her into the darkened house.

He stood still, just inside the door, while Julia lit a lamp. She knew her way around in here, and he didn't. But it took her only a moment to scratch a lucifer into life and hold the flame to the wick of a lamp on a doily-covered, claw-footed table. As she lowered the glass chimney, a warm glow came up and filled the room, which was simply but comfortably furnished.

All the curtains were drawn, including the one over the window in the front door. Longarm took off his hat and then peeled his sodden coat from his body.

"If you've got some place I can put these wet duds, maybe the kitchen . . ."

"Don't stop there."

He looked up at her in surprise. She had taken off his slicker and stood there holding it.

"Beg your pardon, Miss Foster?"

"You're soaked to the skin. And if I'm going to call you Custis, you have to call me Julia."

Longarm shrugged. "All right. But you ain't suggesting—"

"I most certainly am. Take all your clothes off. I'll build a fire in the kitchen stove and warm up that room. I'll have them dry in no time."

She was either the most innocent gal he had run into in a long time . . . or she wasn't so innocent at all. From the merry twinkle he saw in her eyes, Longarm suddenly had a feeling it was the latter.

"Go on in the kitchen and just drop everything on the floor. I'll get you a towel."

Longarm's eyes narrowed as Julia left the room and disappeared down a hallway. He liked to think of himself as a gentleman, but at the same time he was a man who enjoyed the pleasures life had to offer. And Julia certainly seemed to be offering.

Or maybe she was just teasing him. Some gals were like that. Meet a man, get him all hot and bothered, and then slam the door on him. If that turned out to be the case,

Longarm would be sorely disappointed, but he could live with that disappointment.

He went into the kitchen. Enough light came from the parlor for him to see his way around. He placed his hat on the table and hung his coat over the back of a chair. Then he sat down and worked his boots off, leaving them in a corner near the stove.

By the time Julia came into the kitchen carrying a large, thick towel, Longarm had stripped down to the bottom half of his long underwear. Despite the warmth of the evening, his wet skin felt a little cool and clammy.

"You didn't take everything off."

Longarm turned to see her holding the towel. He was still partially dressed, but she wasn't. She stood there nude, her skin soft and creamy in the light from the parlor.

"We just met not much more than an hour ago." The words came out of his mouth in a husky growl.

"I know that." She came closer. "I also know that I wanted you as soon as I saw you come into the café with Marshal Ryan, Custis. Do you know how long it's been since I had a man?"

"I wouldn't have any earthly idea."

"Too long, that's how long! I swear, everybody in this town looks out for me like I'm some sort of innocent little girl, and I can't have *any* fun."

She wasn't a little girl, that was for sure. Her breasts were a good-sized handful each, crowned by large brown nipples that were already erect. Her hips had a womanly curve to them, and her thighs were inviting. Longarm had the urge to run his fingers through the triangle of dark blond hair where her thighs came together and see if she was already wet.

He was willing to bet a hat that she was.

"If you're sure this is what you want . . ."

"I am."

"Well, then, it's always been my policy to oblige a lady."

"Just don't treat me *too* much like a lady." Her voice was a whisper as she came closer to him and started drying his muscular torso with the towel. She leaned in closer, came up on her toes, and kissed him.

Longarm returned the kiss, which started out sweet and gentle but quickly grew hotter and more urgent. After a moment, Julia stepped back, draped the towel around his shoulders, and hooked her fingers inside the waistband of his underwear. She pulled the garment down over his hips and thighs, freeing his already hard cock. It sprang up and jutted out from his groin.

As he stepped out of his underwear, she took the towel and began using it to dry him from the waist down. That put his manhood right in her face as she knelt in front of him. Her honey-colored hair brushed softly against the sensitive flesh and made him tighten his jaw. Julia reached between his legs with the towel and worked it back and forth.

Then she looked up at him with an impish smile on her face. "How much of that big thing do you think I can get in my mouth, Custis?"

"I don't reckon either of us will be satisfied until you find out."

"Oh, I intend for you to be satisfied . . ."

With that, she dropped the towel, wrapped both hands around his long, thick shaft, and leaned in to take the head of it into her mouth.

Longarm closed his eyes. A long sigh of pleasure came from him as her lips closed around him and a delicious warmth enveloped him. He had once heard a fella say that the worst French lesson he'd ever gotten from a gal was still damned good, and there was a lot of truth to that. His arousal grew as Julia's tongue swirled wetly around the head of his cock.

She steadied herself with one hand on his hip and slid

the other between his legs to cup his balls. Longarm spread
his feet a little to brace himself. He rested his hands on her
bare shoulders as she took more of his shaft into her mouth.
Her head began to bob up and down slightly as she established a gentle rhythm.

He could have stood there and let her suck him until he
exploded down her throat, but he knew that wasn't what she
wanted. After a while he urged her to her feet and drew her
into his arms, molding her body against his in a tight embrace as he kissed her again. Their tongues fought a heated
duel, thrusting and stroking against each other.

She finally broke the kiss, stepped back, and grabbed his
hand. "The bedroom's in here!"

She practically galloped in there, dragging him after her.
Longarm was a lot bigger than her, of course, and could
have stopped her, but he went along willingly.

When she reached the bedroom, she was trembling with
need so bad she had trouble lighting the lamp. Longarm suggested they could do it in the dark, but she didn't like that
idea.

"I want to see you, Custis. I want to watch you while
you're making love to me."

That sounded like a decent idea to Longarm, too, since
Julia was so pretty, so he took the lucifer she was trying to
light, snapped it to life with an ironhard thumbnail, and
held the flame to the lamp's wick. It caught and flared up.
He turned it down so that the light it gave off was dim.

That was enough for him to be able to see her sleek,
nude beauty. She clutched at him and drew him down onto
the bed with her. As she lay on her back and spread her
legs, he gave in to the impulse he'd had earlier and stroked
his fingers through her bush. When he reached her opening,
his middle finger delved easily into it. She was wet, all
right. Drenched, in fact, and ready for him.

He moved into position between her thighs and brought
the head of his cock to the fleshy folds of her sex. She

reached up and caught hold of his shoulders as her hips moved under him, wordlessly urging him to enter her. His hips flexed powerfully as he drove forward, sheathing himself in her.

Julia threw her head back and cried out, not in pain but in pure pleasure. He could tell that from the look on her face. She closed her eyes and turned her head from side to side as she gasped.

"Oh, yes! Oh, yes! Now, Custis!"

Longarm didn't need any more urging. He launched into a steady rhythm, pistoning his shaft in and out of her. She was hot and tight and her interior muscles clasped fiercely around him. Her legs wrapped around his hips and twined together as if she never intended to let him go.

A fella would get mighty hungry after a while, he supposed, but there was something to be said for the idea of spending the rest of his life with his cock buried in Julia Foster's pussy . . .

Her hips bucked as she began to spasm wildly underneath him. That drove Longarm over the edge. He thrust into her as deeply as he could go, then froze as his manhood began to erupt in a series of throbbing bursts. His juices splattered hotly into her, filling her. She jerked and cried out as they climaxed together.

After that peak, he continued to hold her as they both enjoyed the long, leisurely slide down from the crest. He let his shaft soften inside of her until it finally slipped out. Then he rolled onto his back and drew her against him. She buried her face against his shoulder.

"Finally. Finally I'm a woman."

Longarm drew in a sharp breath at those whispered words from her. "What?"

She laughed softly as she lifted her head. "You didn't know it, Custis, but you just made love to a virgin."

Chapter 8

Longarm's first impulse was to sit bolt upright in the bed and exclaim, "What the hell!"

But he couldn't do that with Julia snuggled against him like she was, so he settled for turning his head sharply so that he could stare at her in surprise.

"You didn't say anything about that. And when I . . . I mean, I didn't feel anything when I . . . Damnit, you know what I'm talking about!"

He wasn't used to being so tongue-tied. It annoyed the hell out of him.

It didn't help matters when Julia laughed softly, either. "You mean you didn't feel my maidenhead break when you put that big cock of yours in me? That's because it wasn't there. Custis, I've been putting anything I could find that was roughly the right size and shape up there ever since I was fourteen."

He didn't know what to say to that, so he just sighed and shook his head.

"You're angry with me, aren't you?"

"Well . . . you should have told me."

"Would you have been here in my bed if you had known I'd never done this before?"

Longarm frowned. She had a point there, and he couldn't deny it.

"Probably not."

"But you enjoyed it, didn't you?"

"Well . . . blast it . . . of course I did."

She sighed in satisfaction and rested her head on his shoulder again. "So did I. So that's all either of us should be worried about, isn't it?"

"There's more to it than that."

"Not right here and right now. Not for me."

"You're liable to feel different about that one of these days."

She laughed and curled her fingers around his now-soft manhood. "I doubt that very seriously. I don't think I could have had a better first time."

Longarm blew out his breath and gave up arguing with her. She was plenty old enough to have known good and well what she was doing. And judging by the skill and vigor and enthusiasm she had brought to the experience, it was obvious she had done a heap of practicing on her own.

Anyway, it wasn't like Julia Foster was the first maiden he had deflowered, as the fancy novelists put it. Such a thing was rare in his experience, to be sure, but not unheard of.

One thing puzzled him, though, and as he lay there holding her, it continued to nag at his brain. Finally he gave in to his curiosity.

"You said the marshal and your boss and the rest of the folks in town sort of look after you?"

"That's right. It's like the whole town adopted me after my folks passed away." Julia chuckled. "Why do you think I've had such a hard time finding a fella who'd bed down with me?"

"I'd figure there were plenty of cowhands and miners who'd plumb admire to have done the deed with you."

"Oh, I'm sure. But Marshal Ryan and Arnie won't let any of them anywhere near me when we might be alone. I have a whole town full of chaperones!"

That was mighty strange, because Ryan had practically pushed Julia into Longarm's embrace tonight. Could be that Ryan had thought Longarm was trustworthy, what with him being a fellow lawman and all. But Ryan certainly hadn't made any mention of how he expected Longarm to keep his hands off Julia.

He couldn't very well ask the marshal about it, either, without giving away what had happened. He didn't want to get on Ryan's bad side when he was relying on the local lawman to try to find out something about Ed Galloway's whereabouts.

He would just have to keep his mouth shut about what had happened tonight, he decided, and hope that Julia would do the same.

In fact, it might be worthwhile to try to make sure she did.

"You weren't planning on saying anything to the marshal about this, were you?"

She pushed herself up on an elbow and stared at him. "Why in the world would I do that?"

"I don't know. I just figured it wouldn't be a good idea if you did."

"You're afraid of him." Julia looked slightly disappointed.

Longarm sat up and frowned. "That ain't it at all. He seems like a good fella, and I'd just as soon not cause him any grief. If he finds out what happened, he's liable to feel like he's got to do something about it."

"Like try to defend my honor?" Julia sat up, too, and looked worried. "I didn't think about that. I was so . . . aroused . . . that I didn't think about much of anything else at all."

Longarm knew how folks could get carried away, so

he nodded. "Yeah. We'll just keep this between ourselves." He felt a mite soiled saying that and wished that for once he had just kept it in his trousers, no matter whose idea it had been or how badly Julia had wanted it.

She drew her knees up and wrapped her arms around them. "I think you should probably go now." Her voice was small. "I wish you could stay all night, but it might not be a good idea. I do hate to send you back out into that rain, though."

"Well, maybe my clothes will be dried out some by now, anyway."

Unfortunately, in their hurry to get to the bedroom, Julia had forgotten to build a fire in the stove as she had said she would, so Longarm's clothes were still pretty damp. Julia was upset about that, but he tried to reassure her that it was fine.

"It don't matter. I won't be wearing them that much longer, anyway. All I have to do is collect my horse and take him down to the blacksmith shop and livery stable. I'm hoping the fella who owns it will let me bed down in his hayloft for the night."

"I imagine he will. His name is Josh Willard, and he's a nice man."

"Most of the folks I've run into in Warhorse seem to be pretty nice."

"They are. I don't know what I'd have done if I'd been left on my own in some other town where people didn't care."

Longarm pulled on the wet clothes, kissed Julia good night, and stepped out into the storm, which continued unabated. The rain still poured down, the thunder still rumbled, and the lightning still flashed and crackled. As Marshal Ryan had commented earlier, it looked like the storm had settled in for the night and wasn't going away any time soon.

The streets were a soggy mess by now. Longarm slogged

along in the mud, often sinking up to the ankles of his black, stovepipe boots. The damp clothes gave him a clammy chill, and goosebumps broke out on his skin.

His rented horse wasn't in any better shape, though. The poor animal had been standing out in the rain for several hours now, and Longarm felt a twinge of regret when he saw the horse standing at the hitch rail in front of the marshal's office. The lamp was off inside, and the office was dark. Ryan had either turned in early, or he had gone somewhere else. Maybe he was making the rounds of the saloons, asking about Ed Galloway, Longarm mused.

He was just reaching for his horse's reins when a shot roared and a tongue of flame licked out from the mouth of an alley across the street. Longarm felt the wind-rip of the bullet's passage, just inches from his ear.

The horse jumped and let out a shrill whinny of pain, jerking its reins loose from the hitch rail. The animal galloped wildly down the street, mud splashing high around its pounding hooves. From the way it was running, Longarm didn't think the horse was hurt too bad. Probably just grazed by the slug that had barely missed him.

But that left him out in the open with no cover and some son of a bitch across the street trying to ventilate him. At least there only seemed to be one bushwhacker, instead of the four who had ambushed Marshal Ryan earlier in the evening.

That was small consolation, though, as another shot blasted. Longarm was already moving, twisting aside and reaching under his slicker to draw the Colt. The second bullet whistled past his head. By then, he had the revolver leveled and triggered it twice.

The .44 bucked in his hand. He wasn't firing high this time. There was no doubt in his mind that the bushwhacker was trying to kill him, so he responded in kind, aiming at the spot where he had seen the muzzle flashes.

At the same time, he ran at an angle across the street.

There was no good cover on this side, so his best bet was to get somewhere that the bushwhacker's bullets couldn't reach.

Another shot roared out, but Longarm was moving too fast and the visibility was too bad for accurate shooting. He didn't know where the slug went, but the important thing right now was that it didn't hit him. With a bound, he leaped onto the boardwalk across the street from the jail and pressed his back against the front wall of a darkened building.

Longarm looked along the wall toward the spot where the shots had come from. He figured there was an alley or some other narrow passage down there where the hidden gunman had lurked. If he saw even a flicker of movement from the spot, he intended to open fire.

There were no more shots, though, and as Longarm blinked rainwater out of his eyes, he didn't see anything moving down there. He edged along the building in that direction, the Colt ready in his hand for instant use.

He reached the corner of the building, and sure enough, there was a narrow space about four feet wide between that one and the next structure. It was as black as pitch in there, of course, and Longarm knew the would-be killer could still be there, just waiting for him to poke his head around the corner.

He wasn't a big enough fool to do that. This was a waiting game now. Cat and mouse of the deadliest sort.

The game was interrupted by heavy footsteps hurrying along the boardwalk. Longarm glanced up and saw the bulky shape of a slicker-clad man coming toward him at a fast trot.

"Hold it! Stay back, mister!" Longarm couldn't let some innocent townie blunder right into the middle of a gunfight.

The other man on the boardwalk wasn't some innocent citizen, though. He stopped short and drew a gun from under his slicker.

"Long?"

Longarm recognized Marshal Pat Ryan's voice. "Yeah, it's me, Marshal."

A shout came from up the street as several men hurried toward them to see what the commotion was about. Ryan waved them back, identifying himself and calling a command for them to stop, then turned back to Longarm.

"What is blazes is going on here?"

"Another ambush, only I was the target this time, not you. Somebody threw down on me from this little alley."

Ryan's voice lowered. "Are they still in there?"

"Your guess is as good as mine."

Ryan waited there for a moment, then gave a resigned grunt. "Hell with this. Cover me."

Before Longarm could say anything, Ryan twisted around the corner so that he faced the dark passage, crouching low and swinging his gun from side to side. No shots erupted.

Longarm wasn't all that surprised. Ryan's arrival had made the odds two to one against the bushwhacker, and there were townspeople close by, too, who might take a hand. Seeing that his attempt to kill Longarm had failed, the unknown gunman had most likely fled.

Ryan straightened and holstered his gun. He put a hand inside his slicker and dug around for something.

"I don't know if I can get a match to light in this downpour, but I'll give it a try. I want to have a look-see back here."

Ryan cupped his hand over the lucifer to protect it, struck it with the thumbnail of his other hand, then shielded the match as he lifted it so that the flame's glare spread over the narrow alley.

Longarm kept his gun in his hand as he stepped around the corner to look along the passage with Ryan. Other than some trash littering it here and there, there was nothing to be seen. Longarm saw some places in the mud that had to be footprints, but the floor of the alley was too boggy for the markings to be distinct.

"He's gone."

Longarm nodded in agreement with Ryan. "Seems to be."

"You get a look at him?"

"Not even a glimpse."

"Well, that's a damned shame. I'm wondering if he was one of the bunch that bushwhacked me earlier. They could have seen you well enough to recognize you again, and one of 'em might have come back to settle the score with you for interfering in their plans."

That theory seemed a mite far-fetched to Longarm, but he supposed that he couldn't rule it out. "You ever figure out who those hombres were?"

Ryan shook his head as he dropped the burned-out match in the mud. "No. I haven't had any run-ins lately with anybody who might want to blow holes in my hide. It's a plumb mystery to me."

It was a mystery to Longarm, too, and he didn't like mysteries. They had a way of making a fella dead if he wasn't careful.

"You really think one of those varmints slipped back into town?"

Ryan waved a hand to indicate the storm going on around them. "Hell, General Custer and the whole damned Seventh Cavalry could sneak into town on a night like this if they were still alive!"

Longarm supposed he was right. The rain and the shadows made it hard to see more than forty or fifty yards in any direction. Lighted windows any farther away than that were just formless yellow blobs, and anybody in dark clothing would be damned near invisible on a night like this.

He holstered his gun. "We won't be able to track whoever took those shots at me. Reckon I'll just have to wait for him to try again and plan on getting him next time."

"That's a mite hard on the nerves, isn't it?"

Longarm shrugged. "I'm used to it."

Or as used to it as a man could get, knowing that somebody wanted to kill him.

Chapter 9

Marshal Ryan offered to help Longarm look for his horse, but Longarm told him to go on back to his office.

"The varmint can't have run off too far. He's probably looking for a place to get in out of the rain, if he's got any sense."

Ryan frowned. "I don't like the idea of you wandering around town without anybody to watch your back. For some reason, this storm seems to have brought in a heap of trouble."

They were saved from having to argue anymore by a short, broad hombre who came along the street leading Longarm's rented mount.

"Hey, Marshal, this horse showed up at my stable with a bullet graze on its butt. You have any idea who it belongs to?"

Longarm grinned at Ryan. "See, I told you it'd try to find some shelter."

Ryan shrugged. "Looks like you were right."

Longarm turned to the man, who evidently was the proprietor of the blacksmith shop and livery stable. "That cayuse is mine, old son. I was about to come looking for it. And before that, I was about to come looking for your place. Need somewhere to keep that horse for a day or two."

"I can accommodate you." The man stuck out a blunt, thick-fingered hand. "Josh Willard's the name."

"Custis Long." He inclined his head toward Ryan. "The marshal here will vouch for me."

Ryan nodded. "That's right."

"That's good enough for me. You want me to put some salve on that graze once we're in out of the rain, Mr. Long?"

"I'd sure appreciate it. Got another favor to ask of you as well. I'd be glad to pay extra if you'd let me bed down in your hayloft tonight . . . providing it doesn't leak, that is."

Willard grinned. "Not a drop. I put a new roof on the place back in the spring. Don't want to share a bed at the boardinghouse with a couple of prospectors, eh?"

"Not particularly."

"Hayloft ain't as fancy as the rooms upstairs at Kilroy's." Willard threw back his head and gave a booming laugh. "Not that they're all that fancy. Probably not any more bugs crawlin' around in that straw than there is in a whore's bed, either."

Longarm said good night to Ryan, who walked off in the rain toward the marshal's office while Longarm and Willard headed for the stable. Once they were inside the roomy, high-ceilinged building with its familiar smells of horseflesh, manure, and straw, Willard gestured toward the ladder that led up to the loft.

"I'll tend to your horse. You can climb up there and get those wet duds off, Mr. Long."

"Call me Custis." Longarm sighed. "And I just remembered, I left my bedroll and my other gear over in the marshal's office. I better go get it before Ryan turns in. Wouldn't want to wake him up."

"You got to go back out into that storm?"

Longarm sighed. "It's a pisser, ain't it? Seems like I've gone in and out of that downpour a dozen times this evening."

He left Willard unsaddling the horse and started back up the street. The marshal's office was on the same side as the livery stable.

As he plodded through the rain, Longarm thought about the attempt on his life. There was one man who had a good reason to want him dead: Ed Galloway.

But for Galloway to be the varmint who'd ambushed him a short time earlier, two things had to be true.

First of all, Galloway actually had to be here in Warhorse, and Longarm had no proof that was true, only, as Ryan had pointed out, the week-old word of a stranger.

Secondly, assuming that Galloway *was* here in town, he wouldn't have taken those shots at Longarm unless he knew who the lawman really was and why he had come to Warhorse. As far as Longarm could see, there was no way Galloway could have found out about that.

As he came closer to the marshal's office, Longarm suddenly paused and stiffened, forgetting that speculation for the moment. He saw an indistinct shape flitting from shadow to shadow across the street. As he watched, another form appeared and ran across the street beyond the marshal's office. Longarm's hand slid under his slicker and closed around the butt of his Colt as he watched and spotted two more men closing in on the building.

Thoughts raced through his head. He wasn't sure Ryan was right about the man who had shot at him being one of the group that had ambushed the marshal earlier. But it sure looked like that bunch really had come back, and now they were surrounding Ryan's office. Longarm knew they couldn't be up to anything good.

He drew back into a deeper patch of shadow as his gun came out of its holster. The rain drowned out the whisper of steel on leather. Minutes passed as Longarm watched the marshal's office and tried to count the men sneaking around it. That was difficult because he couldn't see well.

There were more than the half a dozen who had been in town earlier, though. He estimated at least twice that many men now surrounded the building. A faint light glowed in the window, so Longarm figured Ryan hadn't turned in yet. He wouldn't have any idea of the danger that was closing in on him, though.

It wasn't lightning as much now as it had been earlier, but there were still occasional flashes. One of them ripped across the sky now, and in that split-second glare, Longarm got a good look at three men who were creeping toward the door of the office. They all wore slickers and had their hats pulled down low over their faces.

They all had guns in their hands, too. Reflections of the lightning flickered on the barrels.

Were they going to kick in the door or just stand off and pour lead into the place?

Longarm wasn't going to give them a chance to do either one of those things. He took a deep breath, brought up his Colt, and was ready when the lightning flickered again and thunder rumbled over Warhorse Mountain.

He fired three fast shots, aiming low. His bullets knocked the legs out from under one of the lurkers, who screamed in pain as he toppled off his feet. In the couple of seconds of echoing silence that followed the reports, Longarm bellowed a warning to the marshal inside the office.

"Ryan! Bushwhackers outside! Stay down!"

The other two men on the porch whirled toward him and started blazing away. Longarm had already ducked into a little alcove that sheltered the front door of a business. The bullets whined past harmlessly.

He heard the boom of a shotgun that sounded almost like thunder, but not quite. The fact that Ryan wasn't able to just lie low didn't surprise Longarm. The marshal didn't strike him as the sort of man who would allow anybody else to fight his battles for him. He would be in the thick of any trouble that broke out in his town.

Longarm crouched and risked a look past the edge of the alcove. He saw two men running across the street toward him. Muzzle flame jetted at him, and a slug chewed splinters from the wall above his head. He fired and saw one of the men go over backward as if a giant fist had just smashed into him. The other man fired wildly, the bullets shattering a window to Longarm's right. He took his time coolly lining up the shot and pressed the Colt's trigger again. This slug ripped through the second man's body and spun him off his feet.

Shouts came from down the street. For the third time this evening, what sounded like a small-scale war had broken out in Warhorse . . . and the night was still young. The citizens had to be wondering if the rain had brought madness with it.

More gunfire erupted around the marshal's office, and the shotgun boomed again. Longarm heard running footsteps sloshing through the mud, and when he ventured a look, he saw slicker-clad men running away from Ryan's stronghold. Since they hadn't been able to take the marshal by surprise, getting to him in the sturdy stone building would be difficult. Clearly they had decided that in order to do so, they would have to pay a higher price than they were willing to pay.

They had already left two men behind, cut down in the street by Longarm's bullets. The man he had wounded in the leg was gone, no doubt helped to flee by his companions.

The other two were still sprawled in the mud, though. Some of the townspeople had reached the bodies. Longarm stepped out of the alcove and approached them.

One of the men spotted him coming, gun in hand. "Hey, mister, what the hell?" There was a note of fear and alarm in his voice.

Longarm didn't holster the Colt, but he kept it down at his side. "Take it easy. I'm on the side of the angels. Those varmints and about a dozen more were fixing to attack the marshal's office when I came along and spotted them."

"Who are they?"

"I don't know. Maybe Marshal Ryan will."

Even as Longarm spoke, he saw the door of the marshal's office open, spilling light out into the street. Pat Ryan appeared, carrying a Winchester now instead of the shotgun he had been wielding at close range a few minutes earlier.

"Long? Is that you down there?"

"Yeah. Got a couple of the varmints here, Marshal."

Ryan stepped down from the porch into the muddy street and strode toward the group of men clustered around the bodies. He was hatless and no longer wore his slicker, and he didn't seem to care that he was getting soaked by the hard rain.

"Drag those bodies over there to the porch so we can get a look at them, boys, if you don't mind."

"Sure, Marshal." The men who had come up to check on the shooting had the look of cowboys from one of the nearby spreads. They had probably been drinking in one of the saloons when they heard the shots. They bent, picked up the corpses by shoulders and legs, and carried them over to the marshal's office.

In the light that came through the open door, the dead men had the rough, beard-stubbled look of hard cases, the sort of varmints Longarm had run into hundreds of times during his career as a lawman. He didn't recognize either of them, but after a while, a lot of these owlhoots started to look alike. He turned to Ryan.

"You know them, Marshal?"

Ryan shook his head. "Never saw them before."

"Then why were they and the rest of their bunch sneaking up on the jail?"

"Is that what was going on?" Ryan grunted. "I just heard shots outside, and when I looked out the window somebody started firing at me, so I just grabbed a shotgun and let loose."

More footsteps slogging through the mud made Longarm look around. He saw Dr. Randall Chamberlain approaching, medical bag in hand.

"I heard the shots and thought my services might be needed." Chamberlain stepped up onto the porch, looked down at the dead men, and shook his head. "It appears that the undertaker is the one required, however."

Ryan nodded. "Yeah, Doc, I'm sorry you came out in this rain for nothing."

"No one else was injured?"

"I don't think so." Ryan looked at Longarm. "How about you?"

"I'm fine. They took a few shots at me, but none of 'em came close."

"I suppose I'll head home, then. Good evening, gentlemen."

"Night, Doc." Ryan turned to the cowboys who stood huddled under the porch roof, out of the rain. "Can one of you fellas fetch the undertaker?"

A couple of the punchers volunteered and strode off into the downpour. Ryan told the other men to keep an eye on the corpses and then motioned for Longarm to follow him into the office.

The marshal set the Winchester on his desk and turned a suspicious frown toward Longarm. "I thought you'd gone down to the livery stable to bed down for the night in Josh Willard's hayloft."

Longarm gestured toward his bedroll and saddlebags, which still lay on the floor next to the old sofa under the front window. "I remembered that I left my gear here."

"Well, I reckon that was a lucky thing for me. It looked like those bastards had the place surrounded. I might not have gotten out of here alive if you hadn't come along and spoiled things for them. You *did* just happen to come along?"

Longarm bristled with anger. "What do you mean by that, Ryan? You think I'm tied in somehow with that bunch?"

"They showed up in town not long after you did. And it seems like every time they try something, you're right there to take a hand."

"Are you forgetting that I just killed two of them? Would I do that if they were my compadres?"

"I don't know. I'm asking you."

The two men traded tense glares, but the situation was broken up by one of the cowboys, who stuck his head inside the door to announce that the undertaker was there. Ryan stepped outside to deal with that, while Longarm gathered up his gear.

Both prisoners called from the cellblock, prompting Longarm to go back there. They stood gripping the bars in their cells.

"What the hell's goin' on out there?"

"Yeah, it sounded like a damn war!"

Longarm shook his head. "Nothing to do with either of you fellas, at least as far as I know. Somebody seems to have it in for the marshal."

Dennehy snorted. "More power to 'em, I say."

Coolidge nodded. "Yeah, I got no use for a damn lawdog, either."

Longarm didn't mention the fact that he packed a badge, too. He just told the two prisoners to quiet down and go to sleep, then turned to leave the cellblock.

When he went outside, he saw that the two bodies were being loaded into a wagon by the undertaker and a couple of burly assistants. Ryan stood watching, the rifle tucked under his arm now. He glanced at Longarm.

"Heading back to the stable?"

"Yeah. It's been a long day."

Ryan sighed and nodded. "I just hope it doesn't get any longer. And I wish this damn rain would let up."

Longarm wasn't sure either one of those things was going to happen.

Chapter 10

Longarm made it back to the stable without anybody else taking a shot at him. The way things had been going, he viewed that as something of a surprise.

Josh Willard had finished unsaddling the horse and tending to its injury. The animal was in a stall now, enjoying a little grain that Willard had poured into the feed trough.

The burly blacksmith and liveryman nodded toward the street as Longarm came in carrying his bedroll and saddlebags. "I heard shots a few minutes ago. Everything all right out there?"

"A little ruckus down at the marshal's office. Some men tried to break in there."

Willard's eyes widened. "Really? Were they trying to break out those hard cases Pat locked up this afternoon?"

"Nope."

"What were they after, then?"

That was a good question, thought Longarm. As far as he could tell from the events of the evening, all those gunmen really wanted to do was to kill Marshal Pat Ryan.

But the question remained—why? Some owlhoots just hated lawmen, of course, but this struck Longarm as something more than that. Such a large group wouldn't go to so much trouble trying to kill one badge toter out of sheer cussedness. At least, Longarm didn't think so.

He realized that Willard was looking at him, expecting an answer. He shrugged and shook his head as he hung up his hat and slicker on a couple of nails.

"I don't know, and according to the marshal, he doesn't know, either. A couple of them wound up dead and some others were wounded, though. They took off for the tall and uncut, and with any luck, they won't be back."

Longarm doubted that, even as he said it. His instincts told him that this wasn't over.

"Warhorse used to be such a peaceful town, too."

"Ryan's good about keeping law and order?"

Willard nodded emphatically. "This used to be sort of a wild place, but after Pat showed up a couple of years ago and took the marshal's job, he's settled it down considerable. He's not one of those gunfighting town tamers who sometimes draw even more trouble. He's just tough, plenty tough, and it didn't take long for the miners and the cowboys hereabouts to figure that out. He busted a few heads and threw a heap of 'em in jail the first few months, and since then most of the boys take it easy when they come to town."

"With the exception of Coolidge and Dennehy, the two who are locked up now."

Willard snorted. "Those two are just loco. They've been spoilin' for trouble ever since they showed up in Warhorse, and today they finally got it."

Longarm thought about what the liveryman had said. "Ryan's been the marshal here for two years?"

"Yeah, about that long. I don't remember exactly when he came to town."

"But he's not from these parts?"

Willard shook his head. "Not that I know of. And I've been here nigh on to fifteen years. Came here not long after the war. Were you in that?"

"Yeah, but I disremember which side I fought on." That was Longarm's usual answer. He had no desire to fight the war all over again, like some hombres still did. As far as he was concerned, the Late Unpleasantness could stay well in the past.

Willard laughed. "I know what you mean. I don't even think about it much these days."

They chatted for a few more minutes about Warhorse, and Longarm got the idea that everybody in town loved Pat Ryan, even the ones the marshal had arrested and put behind bars at one time or another for drunkenness, fighting, and assorted hell-raising. According to Willard, Ryan was the best lawman Warhorse had ever seen.

That was interesting. It didn't sound like Ryan had many enemies . . . and yet, someone had tried to kill him twice tonight.

Longarm said good night, then and climbed up the ladder to the loft, taking his bedroll and saddlebags with him. He had a change of clothes in the saddlebags—jeans and a butternut work shirt and fresh long johns and socks—so he stripped off the wet duds, dried himself as best he could, and put on the dry clothes. He spread the soggy garments on a pile of straw.

A rustling from the other side of the loft made him think about rats, but then a sleek yellow tabby emerged from the shadows and sat down to regard Longarm with a look of dignified disinterest. Longarm knew a good mouser when he saw one. He grinned at the cat.

"Howdy, puss. Hope you don't mind some company up here tonight."

The cat ignored him and started washing a paw.

Longarm spread out his bedroll on a layer of hay. After this long, eventful day, it felt good to stretch out and listen to the rain hitting the roof of the stable. It was miserable weather if you had to be out in it, but if you were inside, snug and dry, it was damn near perfect weather for sleeping.

At least, it would have been if somebody out there hadn't started screaming.

Longarm sat bolt upright as he heard the cries. That was a woman's voice. He didn't think she sounded like she was hurt, but she was definitely terrified. He pulled on his muddy boots, then grabbed his gun belt as he got up and buckled it on as he headed for the ladder.

The lamp down below in Josh Willard's office was turned low, but it gave off enough light for Longarm to be able to make his way down the ladder quickly. By the time his feet hit the hard-packed dirt floor of the stable, Willard had emerged from the office with a look of alarm on his face.

"You hear that? Sounds like some gal's mighty upset about somethin'!"

Longarm grabbed his hat and slicker. "Yeah, and I just got good and comfortable, too."

He couldn't sit by and do nothing while a woman was that scared and upset, though. The good Lord just hadn't made him that way. He tugged the Stetson down tight on his head, buttoned up the slicker, and ventured back out into the rain.

Willard stood in the open doorway behind him, not following. Longarm didn't blame the blacksmith.

This was getting damned old, he thought. If it kept up much longer, he was liable to start growing gills and fins.

The screaming was coming from somewhere down around the marshal's office. Somehow that didn't surprise Longarm at all. Nearly all the violent hoopla that had erupted in Warhorse tonight had centered around the marshal's office. Longarm spotted a figure standing in the center of the street. He realized with a shock that it was Della McKittredge, the pretty widow who ran the newspaper.

"Marshal! Marshal Ryan! They have him! They have Jasper, and they say they'll kill him if you don't come out!"

What in blue blazes was going on here? Longarm broke into a run toward Della.

She must have seen him from the corner of her eye, because she whirled toward him suddenly and held out a hand as if pushing him back.

"Stop! Don't come any closer! They said I couldn't bring anybody back with me except Marshal Ryan!"

Longarm threw on the brakes. He didn't know who had Jasper, but he had a mighty bad feeling about it. He could tell by looking at Della how frightened she was. Her hair was soaked and plastered to her head by the rain. Her dress was sodden as well and the hem was dark with the mud that it had been dragged through. Della's eyes were wide with fear.

"Stay back, Marshal Long, please!"

Longarm grimaced. If anybody was listening—and chances were, they were—then the fact that he was a lawman was no longer a secret. He had a hunch that it didn't matter all that much, though. His gut told him that any plans he'd made had already gone out the window.

"Take it easy, Mrs. McKittredge. Tell me what's wrong, and I'll do everything I can to help."

Della shook her head. She had the look of a panicky animal now, ready to either bolt or fight, and she didn't really care which.

"There's nothing you can do. They want the marshal to surrender to them. That's the only thing that will save Jasper's life."

"Who has your boy?"

"I . . . I don't know. Bad men. A dozen or more of them. They . . . they're wearing masks. They broke into the newspaper office and grabbed Jasper before I knew what was going on. One of them . . . one of them said for me to fetch the marshal, or they would . . . they would k-kill Jasper . . ."

Her voice died away in a moan of despair.

Longarm wanted to tell her again to take it easy, but he knew it wouldn't do any good. Della was in the grip of utter terror, and from the sound of what she had told him, justifiably so. Longarm had no doubt that the men who had kidnapped Jasper McKittredge were the same ones who had tried twice now to kill Ryan. Those attempts had failed, so they were going at it a different way. They were going to use an innocent boy as a hostage against the marshal.

"We won't let them kill Jasper." Longarm made his voice as calm and steady and reassuring as he could. "Your little boy'll be just fine, ma'am. I'll see to that."

"But you can't!" Panic and desperation grew stronger in her tone. "Pat's the only one who can, and he won't even come out!"

That puzzled Longarm. A light burned in the front window of the marshal's office. Ryan must have heard Della's plaintive cries. Longarm had heard them all the way down the street at the livery stable, even over the rain. Those screams had had an edge of mortal terror that cut right through the other sounds in this stormy night.

"Do you know he's in there?"

Lightning flashed and thunder rumbled. The glare revealed Della's wet, stricken face for a second.

"I saw his shadow moving around on the shade. But he won't answer me. He just won't answer!"

That was more than puzzling. If Pat Ryan was the stalwart lawman that everybody in Warhorse seemed to think that he was, wouldn't he move heaven and earth to save an innocent little boy? If something was holding him back, it had to be mighty strong.

"The men who have Jasper . . . they gave you a message for the marshal, didn't they?"

"They . . . they said to tell him that they would meet him at the bridge. That he should come alone. That . . . that they would let Jasper go if Pat tells them what they want to know."

Longarm drew in a deep breath. Those mysterious strangers didn't want Ryan dead. They wanted *information* from him.

Information first, then, more than likely, revenge. When they found out what they wanted to know, then they would kill him.

"What am I going to do?" Della's voice shook. "If Pat doesn't go down to the bridge, they'll kill Jasper!" She hesitated. "But if he does go, in the end they'll kill him, won't they? I think I knew all along that's what they wanted."

"Maybe. Maybe not. But your boy's life is at stake . . . and I reckon maybe I've got an idea how to get Ryan out of there."

Della took a step toward him, hope and fear mingling on her face as she raised a hand.

Longarm turned toward the marshal's office, though, and raised his voice in a shout. "Galloway! Come on out, Galloway! You can't keep hiding in there!"

Chapter 11

For a long moment, there was no response from the marshal's office. Longarm stood there staring at the building, while Della gaped at him.

Then a crack of light appeared at the edge of the door. It swung back slowly, and the shape of Marshal Pat Ryan—or rather, Ed Galloway, train robber and murderer—appeared there holding a rifle, silhouetted against the lamp glow.

"How long have you known, Custis? It can't have been long. You've only been in Warhorse a few hours."

Was that all it was? It seemed longer than that, thought Longarm. But Galloway was right.

"That don't matter now. What's important is that your old gang is holding an innocent boy hostage."

Galloway looked past Longarm. "Della, I'm sorry—"

"Sorry!" She surged forward. "You lie to us all this time about who you really are . . . you bring all this trouble down on our heads . . . you put Jasper's life in danger, and all you can say is that you're *sorry*?"

Galloway's face hardened. "I never meant for any of this to happen."

"No, you were just looking for a place to hide out until the manhunt for you died down." Longarm moved a step closer to the office, then stopped as the barrel of Galloway's Winchester swung toward him. "How the hell did you wind up pinning on the marshal's badge and deciding to stay here?"

"Like you said, that doesn't matter now. We have to figure out what we're going to do about this."

"I'll tell you what you're going to do." Della was practically screaming again by now. "You're going to go down there to the bridge and save my little boy's life!"

"That's what they want me to do? Come down to the bridge? You know if I save Jasper's life, it'll be at the cost of my own."

Della drew in a ragged breath. "I didn't think I'd ever say this, Pat, or whatever your name really is, but right now I don't care about your life." Her voice became a wail. "I just want my little boy back!"

"You know, everybody in this town's been telling me what a fine lawman you are." Longarm's words were inexorable. "You're right, I don't reckon it matters how that came about. If there's any truth to it, Galloway, you know what you've got to do." He paused. "And I'll help you."

That brought a look of surprise to Galloway's face. "Why would *you* help *me*? You came to Warhorse to either arrest me or kill me yourself, remember?"

"That was before your old partners grabbed that youngster."

Galloway stood there staring at him for so long that Longarm thought Della might start screaming again. Then Galloway took one hand off the rifle he held and lifted it to his face. He scrubbed the hand wearily over his features.

"You're right." He motioned for them to come up onto the porch, out of the rain. "How are we going to do this, Marshal?"

Longarm took Della's arm and helped her through the mud to the steps. He felt her trembling as he touched her.

When they were on the porch, he faced Galloway. "They

said for you to come alone, but on a night like this, how are they going to know the difference? I'll bet that once you get out of town, you won't be able to see much more than a hand in front of your face."

"Don't underestimate Hawley. He's a tricky son of a bitch."

"Not Noah Hawley?"

Longarm knew the name from numerous wanted posters he had seen, although he had never run into the man himself. Noah Hawley was wanted for assorted train and bank robberies in Texas and New Mexico, as well as a couple of murders. Longarm had never heard anything about him riding with Ed Galloway.

"One and the same." Galloway must have been reading Longarm's mind. "That *Colorado Flyer* job was the first time we ever worked together . . . and the last."

"He took over the gang after you double-crossed them and kept all the loot from that job for yourself?"

Before Galloway could answer, Della ran out of patience. "Are you going to stand around here talking, or are you going to *go get my son back*?"

Galloway lifted a hand toward her. "Don't worry, Della, I'm going to see to it—"

She stopped him cold. "You can call me Mrs. McKittredge. I obviously don't know you nearly as well as I thought . . . Mr. Galloway."

The outlaw-turned-lawman looked pained. "I never meant to hurt you or anybody else in this town."

"What you meant doesn't matter. You brought your trouble down on us."

Galloway nodded. "You're right about that. And it's up to me now to make things right. You must be chilled, the way you're soaked. Go on inside and sit by the stove and dry off a little."

"I don't care about that!"

"I know you don't." Galloway started to reach out, as if

he were going to touch her arm and try to steer her into the office, but then he must have thought better of it. He dropped his hand. "But Marshal Long and I have some talking to do."

For a moment longer, Della stood there glaring at him, managing to look sad and scared and angry all at the same time. Then she gave him a curt nod and started toward the door.

"Just don't take too long. I don't know how much patience that man has."

Once Della was inside with the door closed, Longarm faced Galloway. "You know Hawley. Is he going to kill the boy no matter whether you cooperate with him or not?"

Galloway sighed. "Probably. I could tell right away that he was loco. Kill-crazy. But smart, too. That's why he used my name when he gunned down that conductor."

"What?" Longarm frowned. "You didn't shoot Cullen Johnson?"

"All you've got to go by is my word, but I swear I didn't, Marshal. Hawley told him to go tell the express messenger to open up, and when the conductor refused, Hawley shot him. He yelled out, 'That'll teach you to hop when Ed Galloway gives you an order.' Because we were all wearing masks, none of the witnesses knew any different. Then Hawley turned and looked at me and laughed, like he was as pleased with himself as a little kid who's just pulled some prank." Galloway shook his head. "I knew right then I had to get away from the crazy son of a bitch."

That description of Hawley didn't sound very promising, considering that he was the one who now held Jasper McKittredge prisoner. Longarm felt a pang of fear for the boy, but he shoved it aside. His thinking had to remain cool and steady if he was going to have a chance to save Jasper.

"So from the sound of it, Jasper won't be in any more danger if we don't cooperate with Hawley than he already is if we do."

Galloway nodded. "That's the way I see it. Of course . . . Jasper's not my son." He sighed. "I'd started to hope that maybe someday . . ."

"Save that." Longarm's voice was curt. "How many men does Hawley have?"

"We've accounted for a few of them, but there are still at least a dozen with him, I'd guess."

Those were pretty bad odds. The only thing on Longarm's side was that he might be able to take them by surprise. With luck, he might even be able to dispose of a few of the outlaws before they knew what was going on.

He thought about everything he had seen as he approached the town that afternoon. With the almost sheer, clifflike slope of the mountain behind the town to the west, and the pair of arroyos that ran to the north and south of the settlement, only to merge east of there, it was almost like Warhorse was on an island. Longarm was willing to bet that by now, those washes weren't dry anymore. They probably had pretty swift currents running in them, as the runoff from the mountains was channeled into them.

"Is there any way across those arroyos other than the bridge?"

Galloway shook his head. "Not really. When they're dry, there are dozens of places where you can take a horse down one bank and up the other. But they won't be dry now."

"So the only way out until the water goes down is the bridge."

"That's right."

Longarm rubbed his jaw and frowned in thought. "If that's where Hawley and his bunch are waiting for you, they've got us bottled up good and proper. What about over the mountain? There are mines up there, so there have to be some trails."

"Not any that you can use in weather like this. They'll all be so slick now from the rain that a rider couldn't make it up them, let alone a wagon or something like that."

No matter how hard he thought, no other plans came to Longarm. "Seems like the only thing we can do is take on that bunch . . . and win."

"At six-to-one odds."

"Well . . ." Longarm grinned. "I didn't say it was gonna be easy."

They quickly agreed that Galloway would go to the bridge as his old partner Noah Hawley had demanded. While he was doing that, Longarm would circle around and follow the arroyo, approaching the bridge and the outlaws that way.

"If I could grab the boy and get him away from that bunch, I don't think they could follow us in this storm. It's gonna be up to you to keep them distracted long enough for me to be able to do that, Galloway."

"If you manage to get your hands on Jasper, don't worry about me. I'll slow them down and do as much damage as I can. Head back here to the jail as fast as you can. It's probably the sturdiest building in town. We'll close the shutters over the windows before we go. They're thick enough to stop most bullets. You can fort up in there and hold them off."

Longarm knew that Galloway was talking about sacrificing his own life in order to save Jasper. He didn't try to argue the man out of it.

"For how long? Hawley's liable to lay siege to the place."

Galloway shook his head. "He won't be able to do that. There are too many people in town who have guns and know how to use them. There are always a few cowboys around, and the boardinghouse is full of miners. They won't let a gang of owlhoots tree the town."

Longarm hoped Galloway was right about that. He'd been the marshal here for two years. He ought to know the citizens of Warhorse pretty well by now, Longarm told himself.

"We'd best tell Mrs. McKittredge what we're doing."

Galloway sighed. "You're right. I'd almost rather face up to the guns of Hawley and the rest of them."

"You'll be doing that soon enough."

The two of them went into the office and found Della pacing back and forth. She turned sharply toward them as they walked in.

"Well? Are you going to do anything? Or are you going to let those men kill my son?"

Galloway set the rifle on the desk. "We're going to get Jasper right now." He reached for his hat and slicker. "Don't worry, Del—I mean, Mrs. McKittredge. You have my word that we won't come back without him, safe and sound."

Galloway's promise probably had some truth to it, Longarm thought.

Because if they didn't come back with Jasper, it would probably mean they were both dead.

Chapter 12

Longarm and Galloway left the marshal's office a few minutes later. Longarm had tucked an extra pistol behind his belt and carried one of the Winchesters from the rack in the office. Galloway was similarly well armed. If they needed more firepower than what they had, chances were they were doomed anyway.

Galloway nodded toward the livery stable. "I don't know if Hawley has somebody watching the place or not, but he's smart enough that he might. Go back down to Willard's like you're turning in for the night and wait a few minutes, then slip out the back and head north. You'll come to the arroyo pretty quick, and then you can follow it around to the bridge. I'll try to time it so that I get there about the same time you do."

That plan made sense to Longarm. "How are you going to distract Hawley and the others?"

"Don't know yet. I'll have to figure that out when I get there. But if any shooting starts, I'll be counting on you to find Jasper and get him out of there."

Longarm nodded and started to slap Galloway on the shoulder in farewell, then stopped as he remembered that the man was still a train robber and wanted fugitive. He wasn't sure if he believed Galloway's story about how Noah Hawley had really murdered the conductor on the *Colorado Flyer*, not him, but Longarm had to admit that it sounded like it had the ring of truth.

He lifted his hand in a wave instead, then moved off down the street toward the blacksmith shop and stable. When he glanced back, Galloway was already invisible in the rain-drenched shadows.

Longarm had a worried moment as he wondered if Galloway would really keep his promise to go to the bridge and face up to the men who had come to Warhorse looking for him. Maybe Galloway would flee into the night instead and not give Jasper McKittredge's fate a second thought. The man was an outlaw, after all, even if he had spent the past couple of years evidently living a law-abiding life. More than that, actually. Galloway, in his pose as Marshal Pat Ryan, had upheld the law.

Longarm didn't think Galloway would double-cross him as long as Jasper was in danger, but in the end, all he could do was have faith, he decided. He reached the livery stable and ducked into the barn through one of the double doors that was partially open.

Josh Willard was waiting for him. "What was all that ruckus down the street? Somebody was sure carryin' on."

Longarm liked the liveryman and blacksmith, but he wasn't sure he wanted to trust Willard with the news of what was going on in Warhorse on this stormy night. The townspeople might need to know later on that there was a gang of vicious outlaws nearby, but spreading the word now could cause an unnecessary panic.

"Some woman was upset about something and wanted to talk to the marshal. That's all I really know. I stopped off at one of the saloons for a drink on my way back."

He almost wished that were true. A shot of Maryland rye would go down mighty nice right about now, he thought.

"Town sure is crazy tonight." With a shake of his head, Willard went back into the office and closed the door.

Longarm couldn't argue with that sentiment. Warhorse had looked peaceful as he approached the settlement that afternoon, but it had turned out to be anything but.

He climbed to the loft, waited a couple of minutes, and then looked down into the main part of the stable. No light showed around the edges of the office door. Willard had blown out his lantern and turned in for the night.

Quietly, Longarm went back down the ladder. He struck a lucifer with his thumbnail and cupped his hand around the flame to guide him as he made his way to the barn's rear door. He didn't open the door until he had snuffed out the match and utter darkness closed in around him. Then he slipped out into the night. Rain pelted on the crown of his hat.

Galloway had told him to go north when he left the barn, but determining direction on a night such as this wasn't as easy as it sounded. Longarm took a moment to orient himself using his memory of how the town was laid out, and then he trotted off into the darkness.

He didn't know how long it would take him to reach the arroyo, but after several minutes, he paused as an odd sound reached his ears. It was a rushing, roaring noise, loud enough to be heard over the sluicing of the rain. It came from somewhere ahead of him. For a second he was reminded of the sound of a train coming toward him, and that sent a surge of alarm through him. He had almost been trapped in tornadoes on several occasions and knew that they sounded like that. This was somehow different, though, and the storm that had settled in over the mountains and the town didn't strike him as the sort to contain a cyclone in it.

There was nothing he could do but keep going. The roaring sound grew louder, and suddenly he realized what it was. He stopped short as lightning flickered overhead, revealing that he was only about twenty feet from the edge of the arroyo.

Galloway had been right: the dry wash wasn't dry anymore. In fact, it was a raging torrent of cascading water. Longarm caught only a glimpse of it in the lightning flash, but that was enough to tell him that Warhorse was now enclosed by a roaring river that threatened to escape the banks of the arroyo.

He wasn't surprised. Flash floods were common whenever a storm erupted in this normally dry country. Men had been known to drown in the middle of a desert.

Longarm knew that if he had stumbled into that flooded wash, he would have been swept away with little or no chance to save himself. That flash of lightning had been lucky indeed.

He turned to his right. That would take him toward the bridge. Keeping the roaring torrent on his left was easy. The noise would warn him if he got too close, and if the sound of it began to fade, he would know that he was veering off from where he needed to go.

Suddenly, he spotted a light up ahead that wasn't a lightning flash—or a spurt of flame from a gun muzzle. Instead, it was a steady yellow glow that had to come from a lantern of some sort. Some lanterns were completely enclosed except for an air hole on the bottom of them, so they could burn even in the middle of a rainstorm like this.

That light had to be coming from Hawley and his men. Nobody else would be out and about on a night like this.

Stealthily, Longarm moved closer and saw that the man with the lantern stood at the end of the bridge nearest to Warhorse. There were a couple of men with him.

And Jasper McKittredge was there, too, a small, forlorn figure in the light cast by the lantern. One of the man had a hand clamped on the boy's shoulder to prevent him from trying to run away.

Longarm crouched behind a large rock and studied the

situation. The rest of Hawley's gang, along with the horses, waited on the far side of the bridge. Longarm figured that Noah Hawley himself was one of the men on this side of the bridge, probably the one holding Jasper.

Eyes narrowing against the rain, Longarm pondered his next move. He might be able to put a bullet from his Winchester into the head of the man with his hand on Jasper's shoulder. If he could kill that hombre, he could call out to Jasper and tell the youngster to run. If Jasper dashed off into the darkness fast enough, none of the other outlaws would have a chance to stop him.

Would losing their hostage be enough to make the gang give up its objectives? Longarm sort of doubted that. They wanted vengeance on Ed Galloway for double-crossing them. Even more, they wanted the gold he must have cached somewhere after the *Colorado Flyer* holdup. Even though Galloway hadn't actually admitted that he had kept the loot for himself, Longarm knew that had to be the case. The rest of the gang wouldn't have gone to the trouble of hunting him down just because they wanted revenge. That much effort required a profit motive.

So simply freeing Jasper wasn't going to end the trouble. The citizens of Warhorse would still have to deal with the outlaws, and that would mean innocent lives lost. Longarm was sure of it.

What he needed was a way to cut the gang off from the settlement.

It looked like nature might provide that way. He watched as the bridge trembled under the onslaught of floodwater against its pilings. The water had risen so that it was only about three feet under the floor of the bridge. If it continued to rise, there was a good chance the flood would wash away the span.

Suddenly, the man holding on to Jasper reached under his slicker and drew his revolver. Longarm stiffened as he watched the outlaw press the muzzle of the gun to the boy's head. They began backing toward the center of the bridge. Longarm heard a voice call out, although he couldn't make out the words, and then Ed Galloway strode into the edge of the light cast by the lantern.

Longarm stole closer, and when Galloway spoke, he was able to make out the words over the sound of the rain.

"Let the boy go, Noah! He doesn't have anything to do with this, and his ma's worried about him!"

"She damned well ought to be worried!" The harsh voice came from the man holding the gun to Jasper's head, confirming Longarm's hunch that he was Noah Hawley. "I'll blow the little bastard's brains out if you don't give me what I want, Ed!"

"You hurt him and I'll kill you!"

Hawley laughed. "We're a long way past the point where threats from you worry me. You've lost whatever edge you once had, Ed. You've been sitting here in this backwater town for two years, pretending to be a law-abiding citizen. And it's even worse than that! You're the damn marshal of the place!"

The barrel of the rifle in Galloway's hands rose slightly. "That means it's my job to keep the peace and keep the citizens safe, whatever it takes. That means . . . I'll give you the damn gold."

The men on the far side of the bridge pressed forward slightly at the mention of the gold. The gang had taken a small fortune off that train, enough gold to make every one of them a rich man.

Galloway wasn't through. "I'll take you to the place I hid it, and after you've got the gold, you can do anything you want to me."

"And what do you want in return?"

"You know what I want. Let the boy go."

Hawley and the two outlaws with him, along with Jasper, had reached the center of the bridge. Longarm didn't like the way the span kept shaking under the onslaught of the flood. Hawley and the others had to feel the bridge trembling under their feet.

"Come on out here, Ed! Then the boy can run home to his ma."

"You let him go first! I don't set foot on that bridge until Jasper's gone!"

"There's a dozen rifles on you, you crazy son of a bitch! What's to stop us from just filling you full of lead?"

Longarm was close enough to see the grim smile that tugged at the corners of Galloway's mouth. "If you do that, you'll never know where that gold is."

That was exactly the answer Longarm expected, and Hawley must have, too. The boss outlaw cursed bitterly.

"All right, you've got a deal!" Hawley took his hand off Jasper's shoulder. "But not exactly the way you said." He leaned closer to the youngster. "Boy, you stand right there until I tell you to move, or I'll kill you! You understand me?"

Longarm saw Jasper's head jerk up and down in a frightened nod.

"Hawley, what the hell are you up to?" Galloway sounded both scared and mad.

Hawley and his two companions began backing toward the far end of the bridge, keeping their guns leveled at Galloway now, although Jasper was still in the line of fire.

"You come on across! When you pass the boy, then he can run for home. We're doing it this way because I don't trust you, Ed." Hawley laughed. "I know what a tricky son of a bitch you can be!"

Galloway hesitated. Longarm knew what had to be going through his head. If he surrendered to Hawley and the rest of the outlaws he had betrayed, he was as much as signing his own death warrant. That might be the only sure way to save Jasper's life, though. Galloway might have pretended to be a honest man for the past two years, but before that he had been a criminal from a young age, committing numerous bank, train, and stagecoach robberies. He had never indicated any willingness to put other's lives above his own back then, although as far as Longarm knew Galloway had never killed anybody except Cullen Johnson . . . and according to Galloway, Hawley had murdered the conductor on the *Colorado Flyer*.

Could a man change that much in two years? Was it really possible that Galloway intended to sacrifice his own life to save the child of the woman he probably loved?

It looked like they were about to find out. Galloway stepped onto the unsteady bridge and started forward.

Chapter 13

Longarm was within twenty yards of the bridge now, but as long as he stayed out of the light from the lantern in the outlaw's hand, he might as well have been a mile away. They couldn't see him. Being careful to keep the rifle and the two pistols out of the mud, he dropped to hands and knees and crawled closer still.

"No tricks, Noah. I promise you, this is what I want to do. It'll be better for everybody, all the way around."

Galloway sounded like he was trying to reassure Hawley, but Longarm suddenly realized that the former outlaw was talking to *him*. Galloway wanted to trade his life for Jasper's. He was telling Longarm not to interfere.

Unfortunately, Longarm didn't have that option. After two years of Galloway being a federal fugitive, Longarm didn't intend to let him just waltz off with a bunch of outlaws and get himself killed. If at all possible, Galloway would stand trial for his crimes. Whether or not the charges included Cullen Johnson's murder could be hashed out later.

Besides, that gold belonged to the United States government, and Uncle Sam still wanted it back. And Ed Galloway happened to be the only one who knew where it was . . .

No, Longarm couldn't just sit back and not interfere. But he wanted to make sure Jasper was safe before he made his move.

The bridge timbers let out a groan that was audible over the rumbling roar of the floodwaters. The bridge wasn't going to make it through the night. Longarm had no doubt of that. He just hoped it wouldn't wash away for a few more minutes. Jasper still stood in the center of it, looking frightened and forlorn with his wet hair plastered to his head.

Galloway reached the boy's side. He paused and reached out with one hand to touch Jasper's shoulder, holding the rifle in his other hand. Even though his voice was low when he spoke, Longarm was close enough to make out the words.

"You run back to my office now, Jasper. Your ma's waiting there for you. Tell her I'm sure sorry I caused all this trouble."

Jasper looked up at the man and shook his head. "You didn't cause the trouble, Marshal. Those bad men did."

"Maybe . . . I'm one of the bad men, too."

Jasper's headshaking became even more vehement. "No, sir! You came out in the rain to save me from them."

"That's enough palaver!" Hawley's shout came from the far end of the bridge. "Get over here, Galloway."

Jasper looked confused. "Why's he keep callin' you that name, Marshal?"

"Never you mind." Galloway squeezed the youngster's shoulder. "Run now, Jasper! Run to your ma!"

He gave Jasper a little push that started the boy toward the near end of the bridge. Jasper broke into an awkward run. The bridge suddenly swayed under him and Galloway.

Longarm's breath caught in his throat as he saw the bridge's movement and heard the timbers groan again. If it collapsed while Jasper was still on it, the boy wouldn't have a chance. The fierce current in the water would sweep him away and drag him under.

The rest of the outlaws had backed off, but Hawley still stood at the end of the bridge, on the span itself. "Damn it, come on, Galloway! I traded you the boy like I promised!"

Galloway looked back over his shoulder and watched as Jasper cleared the bridge and reached muddy but reasonably solid ground. The boy was running hard now, and he didn't slow down as he vanished into the darkness, heading toward town.

Galloway turned back toward the far end of the bridge, heaved a sigh, took a step forward.

Longarm had reached the near end. He stood up, brought the Winchester to his shoulder. "Galloway, get down!"

Galloway twisted around at the shout and dropped into a crouch. Longarm fired past him, cranking off three rounds from the rifle as fast as he could work the lever. He was aiming at Noah Hawley, but judging from the way the outlaw leader ran off the bridge, none of the slugs found their mark.

"This way, Ed! I'll cover you!"

Longarm knelt behind one of the thick beams that anchored the railing on one side of the bridge and threw another shot at the outlaws as Galloway broke into a run toward him, leaning over almost double to make a smaller target of himself.

The outlaws weren't shooting at Galloway, though. They still needed him alive to tell them where the gold was hidden. They concentrated their fire on Longarm instead. Muzzle flashes flickered like a bunch of fireflies, or like the lightning that still crawled in jagged lines through the sky overhead. Bullets chewed splinters from the railing near Longarm and whistled past his head.

"Hold your fire! Hold your fire!" The bellowed command came from Hawley. "You might hit Galloway! Get over there and get those sons of bitches!"

The rest of the outlaws stopped shooting as Galloway

reached the end of the bridge and ran past Longarm. They weren't in any hurry to go charging out onto the shacking, swaying bridge, though.

"Get the horses! Get after them! We'll tear that town down around the bastard's ears if we have to!"

What it came down to was that the outlaws were more afraid of Hawley than they were of the bridge. They grabbed their horses, leaped into saddles, and charged out onto the bridge with Hawley in the lead.

Longarm had started after Galloway. He looked back at the sound of thundering hoofbeats on the wooden planks, saw the outlaws riding across the bridge. Hawley and two of his men reached the near side. Three more mounted outlaws were strung out on the bridge, and the rest of the gang was still on the far side of the arroyo.

The bridge's supports picked that moment to collapse at last under the tremendous pounding of the floodwater.

Longarm and Galloway both stopped for a couple of seconds, transfixed by horror at the scene that was visible in the flickering glare of the lightning. They heard the splintering crash of the timbers giving way and saw the bridge tilt crazily to the right. The two outlaws closest to this end whipped their horses frantically as they tried to get off the bridge before it went down. The third man whirled his mount around in an ill-advised attempt to go back to the other side.

It didn't matter. The three owlhoots were doomed no matter what they did. The surging waters broke over the sagging planks and pummeled them even harder. The flood washed around the legs of the horses. The animals screamed in panic and tried to stay upright, but then the bridge broke apart and fell out from under them. Men and horses were plunged into the raging current.

That had taken only a couple of heartbeats, and the unfortunate outlaws and their mounts were out of sight even faster, swallowed up by the water.

Longarm and Galloway still had problems, though. Hawley and two members of the gang had reached this side of the bridge before it collapsed, and the owlhoots galloped toward them now.

Even worse, Jasper still hadn't reached the town. Longarm could see the lights of Warhorse ahead of them now, and he spotted the boy's small figure silhouetted against them as Jasper hurried toward home.

Galloway must have spotted the youngster, too. "Grab the boy and get back to the jail! I'll slow down Hawley and the others!"

"Hell with that! Jasper knows where he's going. We'll make a stand!"

Longarm skidded to a halt, his boots slipping in the mud as he whirled around and brought the Winchester to his shoulder again. He couldn't see Hawley and the other outlaws all that well, but he slammed a couple of shots in the direction of the hoofbeats from their horses. Colt flame stabbed back at him. With Hawley's plan collapsing, the boss outlaw must have decided that he wanted vengeance on Galloway whether he ever got the missing gold or not. He was willing to risk the shots now.

Hawley had to know as well that since the bridge had collapsed, he and his two companions were trapped over here until the water went down. They might want to recapture Jasper so that they could use him as a hostage to keep them safe from the townspeople.

Longarm wasn't going to let that happen.

"We'll split up! Galloway, you go left, I'll go right!"

Galloway didn't waste time discussing the plan. He just ran off into the darkness to the left. Longarm went the other way.

One of the outlaws came after him. The fella must have eyes like a cat to be able to see him in this murk, thought Longarm. The hoofbeats sounded like thunder as the desperado's horse closed in on him.

Longarm flung himself to the side just as he was about

to be trampled. A muzzle flash or lightning or both ripped through the night. Longarm felt the bullet tug at his slicker as he rolled over in the mud.

He hoped the muzzle of the rifle hadn't gotten plugged. If it had, it might blow up in his hands.

He triggered the Winchester anyway.

The rifle cracked sharply. The outlaw and his horse were practically on top of Longarm. The big lawman saw the man's head jerk backward as the slug caught him and bored on up through his brain. The outlaw flew into the air as the slug exploded out the top of the man's head.

The corpse hit the ground with a soggy splash.

Longarm rolled over and came up on his hands and knees as more shots blasted somewhere close by. The other two owlhoots must have gone after Galloway, because he didn't see either of them bearing down on him. He surged up onto his feet and ran in the direction of the shots.

The muzzle flashes were easy to follow, and Longarm could tell that some of them came from a man on the ground who had to be Galloway. The others were higher because the men firing were on horseback. Longarm lifted the Winchester and sent lead searching through the darkness for the outlaws.

He heard somebody howl in pain but didn't know who it was. Could have been Galloway. More shots rang out. Longarm ran after the muzzle flashes as they moved off.

Suddenly, he tripped over something and went sprawling in the mud. A choked, liquid groan made him twist around on the slick ground and bring the rifle to bear. As lightning flashed, he saw one of the owlhoots lying facedown and realized that one of his shots must have gotten lucky and knocked the man out of the saddle.

Longarm rolled the man onto his back and saw the broad, dark stain on his neck and chest. The bullet had ripped his throat out, and with another gurgling sigh, the outlaw died. Longarm left him there and climbed back to his feet.

"Long!"

The shout made Longarm whirl around. He recognized Galloway's voice as the former outlaw called out again.

"Long, are you all right?"

Longarm hurried in that direction, steering by the sound of Galloway's voice. A moment later, in the glare of another lightning flash, he spotted Galloway standing over the body of a man lying on the ground.

"Galloway!" Longarm hurried up to him. "Is that the last of them?"

"Yeah. Noah Hawley himself."

A groan from the man on the ground told Longarm that Hawley was still alive.

"What about you, Long? Are you hit?"

"Nope. You?"

"I got lucky." Galloway sighed. "I guess you could call it that. None of that lead flying around found me. What about the other two?"

Longarm's answer was curt. "Dead. But the ones on the other side of the arroyo ain't."

Galloway shook his head. "I'm not worried about them right now. They can't get to us until the water goes all the way down, and that'll be tomorrow morning at the earliest, probably longer than that." He prodded Hawley with a booted foot. "Anyway, we've got us a hostage of our own now. Or maybe I should say you've got two prisoners, Marshal, instead of one."

"Let's worry about that later. Right now, I want to get back to the jail and make sure Jasper's all right."

"Yeah. Cover this son of a bitch." Galloway bent down, got hold of Hawley's slicker and shirt, and hauled the outlaw to his feet. Hawley gasped in pain. "I drilled him through the shoulder. He won't be raising any hell for a while."

Galloway gave Hawley a shove that sent the man stumbling toward the settlement. He and Longarm followed closely.

Longarm had managed to keep his hat on, but he was soaked and covered with mud anyway. He didn't have any dry clothes to change into this time, either. But this wasn't the first time in his life he'd faced the prospect of spending a wet, miserable night. At least he wasn't riding nighthawk on a herd of half-crazed cattle that might stampede at any time.

There weren't many lights burning in the windows of Warhorse anymore. Most of the town had turned in for the night, the citizens blissfully unaware of all the ruckus that had been going on. They were sleeping peacefully in their beds, and if they woke, they might lie there listening to the sound of the rain on the roof for a moment before smiling and rolling over to go back to sleep.

Longarm thought about Julia Foster doing that, and a smile tugged at his mouth. If circumstances had been different, he might have moseyed back down to Julia's place and asked her if he could come in and dry off again.

He intended to spend the night in the marshal's office, though, helping Galloway keep an eye on Hawley . . . and keeping an eye on Galloway at the same time. He still didn't know how far he could trust the former outlaw. Galloway had been willing to stand up and do the right thing when it came to saving Jasper McKittredge's life, but would he allow himself to be arrested and taken back to Denver to face trial for his crimes?

As the three men approached the marshal's office, Longarm saw that the door was open, allowing a rectangle of light to fall out into the street.

Galloway prodded Hawley in the back with the barrel of his rifle. "Keep moving. That's where you're headed, right up there."

Hawley growled a curse as he clutched at his wounded shoulder with his other hand. He slogged on through the muddy street, up the steps, across the porch, and through the door. Galloway was right behind him, with Longarm bringing up the rear.

As soon as Longarm stepped through the door, he saw Della sitting on the old sofa with her arm around Jasper. The soaked little boy huddled against her. Longarm was about to smile at them when he noticed how pale and drawn and frightened Della's face was.

He had just enough time to realize that something was wrong when he heard a gun being cocked behind him.

"Don't move, you big bastard. I'd love to blow your brains out."

Longarm recognized the voice. It belonged to Mal Dennehy.

Then something crashed down on the back of Longarm's head, sending him pitching forward into a darkness that was even deeper than the stormy night that hung over Warhorse.

Chapter 14

It was a good thing he had a hard head. That, and his hat had absorbed some of the force of the blow. Longarm thought about those things as consciousness seeped back into his brain.

Unfortunately, none of it helped one damn bit, he realized. His head still hurt like a son of a bitch.

But as he had on other occasions, he embraced that pain. It meant he was still alive. As the memory of what had happened came back, he had plenty of unanswered questions, such as how Mal Dennehy had gotten out of that cell.

Finding out about that could wait. For now he was content to just lie wherever he was and hope that his head would quit spinning soon. He didn't open his eyes or move in any other way. If whoever had clouted him believed that he wasn't a threat because he was unconscious, he wanted them to keep on thinking that he was out cold for as long as possible. That would give him more time for his wits to come back to him, more time to regain his strength . . .

So that when he was ready to make his move, at least he would have more of a chance of it being successful.

He heard voices, but they were still too fuzzy for him to

identify them. Gradually, he came to realize that they were men's voices, and several different men, at that.

Mal Dennehy and Dex Coolidge. That was just logical. But there was another man, Longarm thought.

Noah Hawley.

The pieces began to fall into place in Longarm's brain. The pain was still there, but it didn't keep him from thinking.

Somehow, Coolidge and Dennehy had gotten out of their cells and forced Della to tell them what was going on. Della knew most of the story by now, or at least she did if she'd been paying attention while Longarm and Galloway talked. The two prisoners had probably heard some of it from the cell block, as well. Longarm hadn't even really thought about them being back there while he and Galloway were working out their plans. He'd been too worried about Jasper to think of much else, and so had Galloway.

So when Coolidge and Dennehy got loose, they had taken Della prisoner and waited to see who came back to the jail. Longarm and Galloway had walked right into their trap, prodding Hawley in front of them.

Those two hard cases probably knew there was some stolen gold up for grabs—and they would want at least some of it for themselves in return for helping Hawley.

Longarm had just worked that out when he heard footsteps somewhere nearby. Then cold water splashed in his face, making him gasp and sputter. He couldn't pretend to be unconscious any longer, so he didn't even try. Instead, he sat up, shaking his head to get the water out of his eyes and nose and mouth.

That was a mistake in a way, because the rapid movement made his stunned brain joggle around in his skull and set off fresh explosions of blinding pain. That was what it felt like, anyway. As the pain receded slightly and Longarm's vision cleared, he looked up to see Hawley, Coolidge, and Dennehy standing there.

He was looking at them through iron bars, though. He realized that he was locked up in one of the cells.

Hawley had a bucket in his right hand. His left shoulder was swathed in bandages where Galloway had drilled him. Dennehy held another bucket. Longarm glanced across the narrow corridor and saw Galloway stirring on the floor of the other cell. Water dripped off his face. He had been doused, too.

"I thought you boys might be shamming." Hawley grinned as he spoke. "And hell, you're already wet, so I didn't figure a little more water would hurt anything."

This was the first time Longarm had actually gotten a good look at Hawley. He was a handsome son of a bitch in a way, with a cocksure grin and curly brown hair. He had cold, merciless gray eyes, though, and as Longarm gazed at them, he recognized the eyes of a killer.

In that moment, he knew that Galloway had been telling the truth. It had been Hawley who gunned down the conductor on the *Colorado Flyer* and then cleverly blamed the killing on Galloway. If Galloway had been caught a short time later, no one would have believed his story. He would have been hanged for the murder of Cullen Johnson.

Hell, until just now, *he* hadn't been convinced of Galloway's innocence, thought Longarm. And innocence was a relative term anyway, since Galloway had committed plenty of other crimes.

Not hanging offenses, though.

"Damn you, Hawley." The growled curse came from Galloway in the other cell. He looked groggy, and Longarm figured that he had been knocked out, too.

Hawley laughed. "If I'm damned, you'll be there in hell before me, Ed. I'll be sure to look you up when I get there." He tossed the empty bucket into a corner with a clatter. "You've been lying to the good people of this town all this time. Two years pretending to be an honest, upstanding citizen . . . a lawman, even! . . . when all the time you're just a filthy owlhoot like the rest of us. *Worse* than the rest of us, because you're a double-crosser, too."

"I won't argue with you about what I've done. I had my reasons."

"Yeah . . . you're a treacherous, greedy bastard."

Longarm had started to wonder where Della and Jasper were, since Hawley, Coolidge, and Dennehy were all here in the cellblock. He hoped they had gotten away somehow, although that seemed highly unlikely.

That hope was dashed as he heard an angry shout from Jasper. "Don't you talk that way about the marshal, mister!"

Longarm heard Della trying to hush the boy, even though he couldn't see either of them from where he sat on the floor of the cell. Their captors must have tied up the two of them and left them in the office, he thought.

Hawley continued grinning at Galloway. "You can fool a little kid, Ed. You ought to be mighty proud of yourself."

"I'm not proud of anything, least of all the time I spent riding with you."

"Is that why you double-crossed us and kept all the gold for yourself?"

Galloway stared up at Hawley for a second, then looked away and shook his head. "There's no point in talking about it."

"You're right, there isn't." Hawley drew a gun from the holster on his hip. He must have gotten it from the cabinet in the office. Coolidge and Dennehy were armed again, too. Hawley's grin disappeared. "This is the only point. You tell me where to find that gold, or I'll walk out there and shoot that little boy."

Della had to be able to hear him. She let out a choked scream.

Galloway's lips drew back from his teeth in a snarl. "Go ahead and shoot him. He's not my kid."

"But you were willing to come out to the bridge to save him. He must mean something to you."

"I always planned on double-crossing you, tonight, anyway. I thought I could get the boy away from you safely . . . and I did."

"But you don't care about him or his mama?"

Galloway shook his head. "She's just some widow woman who lives here in town. She doesn't mean anything to me." He hesitated, then overplayed his hand. "You might as well let 'em both go."

Hawley threw his head back and laughed, a hearty but somehow evil sound that filled the cell block. "Oh, Ed, you never were too bright. Letting them go was never going to happen anyway, but it sure as hell won't now. Everybody in here knows you're lying about them not meaning anything to you." He turned to look at Longarm. "You know it, too, don't you, Deputy U.S. Marshal Long?"

That brought a frown of surprise to Longarm's face. As far as he knew, Coolidge and Dennehy weren't aware that he was a federal lawman, so they couldn't have told Hawley. How did the son of a bitch know?

"Didn't expect that, did you? Who do you think is responsible for you being here?"

"How the hell . . ." Longarm couldn't stop the muttered exclamation from escaping.

"It was one of my men who told the law in Phoenix that Ed was here in Warhorse. Just like it was one of my men who spotted him in the first place." Hawley glanced back across the hall at Galloway. "You should've been a little more watchful that day, Ed. Remember Jordy Bennett? You never saw him, but he saw you, right enough. He just happened to stop here for a drink, and who does he see through the saloon window, waltzing along the street with a lawdog's badge on his chest just like he owned the place, but our old pard Ed Galloway. Jordy waited until you were out of sight, then grabbed his horse and fogged it out of here. He came straight to me and told me where you were."

"Why didn't you just come after me?" Galloway sounded

like he couldn't stop himself from asking the question. "Why'd you try to turn me in to the law?"

Hawley sounded a little proud of himself as he answered the question. "I figured you must have been here long enough to get yourself established, since you were wearing a town marshal's badge. If we rode in to get you, the townspeople might try to stop us. Hell, they don't know who you really are, or *what* you are. That was a fight we didn't need." Hawley used the barrel of the gun in his hand to point at Longarm. "So I decided to let somebody else do the work for us. We sicced another lawdog on you, figuring that we'd take you away from him once he'd left town and started back to Denver with you as his prisoner."

It wasn't a bad plan, thought Longarm. It might have even worked if things had broken differently.

Hawley continued his explanation. "We hung around the depot at Phoenix until we saw Uncle Sam here get off the train and go talk to the local law. One of the boys recognized him." The outlaw looked at Longarm again. "You remember Jack Harbin?"

"Ugly son of a bitch with a lazy eye I arrested about six years ago?"

Hawley laughed again. "That's him, all right. You've got a good memory, Marshal. Jack busted out of prison three years into his stretch and joined up with us. He remembers you just like you remember him. Probably even better, since you were responsible for him losing three years behind bars."

"It was his decision to become a no-good owlhoot. He can't blame that on me."

Hawley wasn't listening anymore, though. He had turned back to Galloway.

"So we followed Marshal Long out here and figured to wait for him to leave town with you."

"What if he didn't? What if I'd killed him when he tried to arrest me?"

Hawley shrugged. "Then there'd be a dead lawman and we'd be back where we started. Nothing really lost as far as I'm concerned."

"Why'd you come into town tonight, then? Why didn't you just stay out there where you were?"

Longarm had been wondering the same thing.

Hawley's mouth tightened angrily. "It was that damned storm. I got worried about that arroyo flooding and maybe taking the bridge out. Then we'd have been stuck on the other side. Long might not have even started back to Denver until the bridge was rebuilt. Hell, there were just too many things that could go wrong. I decided not to wait and take the chance." He shrugged again. "Anyway, I figured most of the folks in town would be hunkered down to wait out the storm. I thought we could slip into town, grab you, and then get back out without no one being the wiser."

"You got antsy and acted on impulse." Galloway laughed. "You always were reckless, Hawley. I could tell that about you right away. Couldn't stick to a plan. Couldn't be trusted. You proved that on the *Colorado Flyer*."

"You mean about me shooting that conductor?" Hawley grinned that maddening grin of his again. "What can I say? It came to me, and it seemed like a good idea."

Longarm fought down an impulse of his own—to lunge at the cell door and try to reach through the bars so he could get his hands around that murdering bastard's neck.

"I knew then that I'd never work with you again."

"So that's when you decided to keep the gold all to yourself?"

Galloway looked away. "I told you—"

"Save it. We've all blathered long enough. Just tell me where to find it."

"Or you'll kill the boy?"

Hawley shook his head. "No, I've changed my mind about that." He holstered his gun. "But my two new partners and I are going back into the office and take turns having some fun with that pretty little widow woman you say you don't care about. I reckon you'll be able to prove that, Ed, since you'll be able to hear the whole thing loud and clear."

Chapter 15

Galloway surged up off the floor of the cell and lunged at the door. His fingers wrapped around the iron bars and his face thrust against them as his lips pulled back in a snarl.

"You touch Della and I'll kill you! I swear, I'll make every one of you beg to die!"

Hawley laughed. "That's mighty big talk for a man who's on the wrong side of the bars."

Longarm got to his feet as well. Hawley, Coolidge, and Dennehy were all looking at Galloway now. None of them were paying any attention to him. He moved soundlessly toward the barred door.

"This is between you and me, Noah. Give me a gun and we'll settle it. Hell, just let me out of here and I'll take you on with my fists. But you don't touch that woman."

"If you want to protect her, you'll tell me where the gold is."

Longarm was watching Galloway. He saw the defiance suddenly leak out of the man, saw the despairing slump of Galloway's shoulders. Galloway had probably come to Warhorse with no thought in his head other than protecting himself, hiding out until it was safe for him to move on.

But over time something had changed. He wasn't the same man he had been. He had started to care about other people, about one person in particular.

And that was now his fatal weakness, at least as far as Noah Hawley was concerned.

"All right. I'll tell you. But you have to give me your word that you'll let Mrs. McKittredge and the boy go."

"We can't do that right now, and you know it. They'd run for help right away." Hawley paused. "But I will do this. I swear that if you tell me what I want to know, they'll be safe, and we'll let them go as soon as we're ready to leave Warhorse."

"I'm not asking for anything for myself."

Hawley's lip curled. "That's because you know you won't get it. You're a dead man, Ed, and there's nothing you can do about it. You never should have double-crossed me."

Galloway's shoulders slumped even more. "I know. All I care about is Della and Jasper."

"Where's the gold, Ed?" Hawley's voice was soft with menace.

"There's a little canyon about halfway up Warhorse Mountain. I led the pack horses up there and found a place to cache those bags of gold. It's on the left side, about halfway up the canyon. The wall juts out, but there's a space underneath it, almost like a cave. It's only a couple of feet tall. I shoved the bags up in there as far as I could. They're protected there, and nobody would ever see them if they didn't know where they were."

"How do I find this place, exactly?"

"There are a couple of pine trees on a little shelf about halfway up the canyon wall. The spot where the gold is hidden is just beyond them, at the base of the wall."

Hawley got a cunning look on his face. "You wouldn't be lying to me, now would you, Ed? Trying to trick me some way?"

Galloway glared at him. "It's the God's honest truth. I

wouldn't play games with the life of those two people out in the office."

"Oh, yeah, the woman and the boy." An ugly smile stole over Hawley's face. "You know, Ed, I'm not sure I trust you. I think we'll have our fun with the woman anyway and let her boy watch. Then we'll see if you still tell the same story."

Coolidge and Dennehy all but licked their lips in anticipation when they heard Hawley say that.

Galloway's eyes widened in shock. "I knew I couldn't trust you, you son of a bitch!" He slammed his body against the bars and thrust his right arm between them, the fingers of his hand clawing for Hawley's face. Hawley just laughed and stepped back well out of reach, as did Coolidge and Dennehy.

Which brought Dennehy close enough to the other cell so that Longarm could reach out, grab his shirt, and jerk him back hard against the bars.

At the same time, Longarm thrust his other arm through the bars and looped it around Dennehy's neck. The hard case's head banged hard enough against the bars to stun him momentarily. Longarm reached around Dennehy's body and closed his hand around the butt of the revolver tucked behind the man's belt. He jerked the weapon free.

"Get him!" Hawley shouted the command as he twisted around and tried to bring his own gun to bear. Coolidge clawed at the gun behind his belt as he whirled toward Longarm's cell, too.

The gun in Longarm's hand roared. From this angle, he didn't have a good shot at Hawley, but he was able to put lead into Coolidge as the man's gun came up. Coolidge doubled over as the slug smashed into his belly.

Dennehy writhed in Longarm's grip but couldn't pull free of the arm across his throat. He let out a strangled scream as Longarm jerked him back against the bars again.

At the same time, Hawley's gun blasted. Longarm felt

the shudder that went through Dennehy as the bullet slammed
into him. Longarm shoved the Colt under Dennehy's arm
but held off on pulling the trigger as he realized that if he
missed, the shot might hit Galloway.

Instinct had caused Hawley to step back, and in the
close confines of the cell block corridor, that was a mistake.
Galloway's hands closed on his shoulders, including the
injured one. Hawley screamed in pain. Galloway kept his
grip on that shoulder, pressing down hard on it so that the
agony of the wound immobilized Hawley for a second. That
was long enough for Galloway to double his other hand
into a fist and crash it against the side of Hawley's head a
couple of times. Hawley sagged and dropped his gun. Galloway hauled him back against the bars and looped an arm
around his neck, the same way Longarm was holding the
now-limp Dennehy.

It was obvious that Galloway wasn't just holding Hawley in place, though. He intended to choke the life out of
the owlhoot.

Galloway leaned forward so that his face was against the
bars again, only inches away from Hawley's ear. "You never
should've threatened that woman."

Longarm let go of Dennehy. The man slumped to the
floor and rolled onto his back. Longarm saw the bloodstain
on the front of Dennehy's shirt and the vacant, staring eyes.
Hawley had shot without hesitation, but all he had succeeded
in doing was killing one of his allies.

Coolidge was on the floor, too, curled up in an unmov-
ing ball as a pool of blood spread slowly around him. Longarm was reasonably certain that the second hard case was
as dead as Dennehy.

"Galloway!" Longarm's voice cut across the space between them. "Galloway, don't kill him!"

The urgency in the big lawman's tone must have gotten
through to Galloway. The fierce expression on his face cleared
a little, but he was still grimacing as he looked up.

"Why the hell not? He's got it coming. I ran from a murder charge for two years because of him, and you heard what he said about Della!"

"Yeah, but Dennehy and Coolidge are dead, and I'm betting that Della and Jasper are tied up in the office so they can't help us. Hawley's the only one who can unlock these cells and let us out of here."

The logic of that seemed to penetrate Galloway's rage. A couple of panting breaths hissed between his teeth, then he heaved a long sigh.

"You're right. I see the keys there on Coolidge's belt, but I'm not sure either of us could reach them."

Galloway eased his grip on Hawley's throat. The outlaw drew in a deep, ragged breath. He managed to rasp a curse.

"You . . . you son of a bitch . . ."

Longarm lifted the gun and aimed it between Hawley's eyes. "Get the keys. Unlock these cells."

"Why the hell . . . should I?"

"Because if you don't, I'll let Galloway finish what he started. I've got half a mind to do it anyway and just wait until morning for somebody to come along and let us out."

He would do that if he had to, although he preferred not to. There were risks involved in waiting. He hadn't forgotten that the rest of Hawley's gang was less than half a mile away, on the other side of that flooded arroyo. They still represented quite a threat to the town.

"All right. Tell this loco bastard to let me go."

Longarm gestured with the gun. With obvious reluctance, Galloway released Hawley. Longarm kept the revolver trained on Hawley as the outlaw bent and took the ring of keys from Coolidge's belt.

Longarm stepped back from the door. "Unlock this cell first."

Hawley did so. Longarm motioned him away from the door and then stepped out into the corridor.

Galloway gripped the bars. "Now let me out of here."

"Not just yet."

Galloway looked at Longarm in surprise. "Damn it, Long! What are you doing?"

"You're a federal fugitive, Ed." Longarm backed all way to the open door between the cellblock and the marshal's office. "Hawley, get in that cell I just came out of and close the door."

Hawley gave Longarm a hate-filled sneer, but he did as he was told. Crimson had seeped through the bandages on his shoulder where the struggle with Galloway had started the wound bleeding again, and Hawley's face was haggard with pain. He didn't have much fight in him at the moment.

When the cell door had clanged shut, Longarm told Hawley to toss the keys out into the corridor. Hawley did so. Longarm retrieved them and straightened.

From the door of the other cell, Galloway peered out at him. "You can't do this, Long. I helped you."

"I know that. But like I said, you're a fugitive, and as far as I'm concerned, you're under arrest."

"All right, blast it! I'm under arrest. What if I give you my word I won't try to get away?"

Longarm nodded. "That might be all right. You swear you won't try anything?"

"I swear. And unlike Hawley, my word means something."

Longarm believed him. He stepped over to the door, thrust the key in the lock, and turned it, then stepped back quickly just in case Galloway had been lying to him.

Galloway just pushed the door open and stepped out of the cell. "I want to see about Della and Jasper."

Longarm stepped aside. "I don't blame you."

Galloway hurried out into the office. Longarm cast a glance at Hawley. The outlaw sank down on the bunk in the cell and leaned back against the wall.

"I need a doctor."

"We'll see about that." Longarm nodded at the bodies

of Coolidge and Dennehy. "Gonna need to fetch the undertaker, too."

He went out into the office, where he found Galloway untying Della and Jasper where they sat on the old sofa. As soon as Della's arms were free, she threw them around Galloway's neck and hugged him tightly.

"Oh, Pat, thank God!" Then she drew back with a frown. "But . . . you're not Pat Ryan, are you? You're really this man Galloway. An outlaw."

"I was." Galloway's face was stony, but Longarm saw hurt in his eyes. "Now I . . . I don't reckon I really know who or what I am."

"You're the marshal!" That declaration of support came from Jasper. "I believe you."

Della picked him up and set him on her lap, hugged him, too, and stroked his hair as if she had to touch him to reassure herself that they were both really free. Then she turned to Galloway.

"I'm sorry. It's my fault those men got loose. Coolidge claimed that he was really sick and wanted me to bring the doctor. I . . . I got too close, and he grabbed me. When Jasper came in, Coolidge made me tell him to bring in the keys so they could unlock the cell doors."

"You're not a jailer. You don't have anything to do with varmints like those two." Galloway's voice was gruff with concealed emotion now. "Don't blame yourself for what happened. If it wasn't for me, you never would've been left here alone with them." He stood up and turned to look at Longarm. "What do we do now, Long? The rest of Hawley's bunch is still out there."

Longarm glanced at the window as lightning flashed and thunder rumbled like the sound of distant drums. The rain still pounded down.

"As long as they're on the other side of that arroyo, they can't get to the town."

"They know that Hawley's over here, though, and they know that I'm here. They're not going away."

Longarm shook his head. "No, they're not. As soon as the water goes down enough for them to get across the wash, they'll come looking for him . . . and for you."

"We have to be ready for them. We'll need to warn the townspeople. There are only eight or nine of the bunch left. They won't want to take on a whole town that's armed and waiting for them."

Della spoke up. "Is it all true, Pat? I . . . I can't seem to stop calling you by that name. You really were an outlaw? You really stole some gold from the government and hid it?"

Galloway's face looked like it was carved in stone as he nodded. "It's true. I wish it wasn't. But I was a bad man for a long time, Della. The last two years . . . well, that's just about the only time in my life I tried to live like a decent hombre."

She shook her head. "It's just so hard to believe. Only a few hours ago, things were normal around here. And then that damn storm blew in, and nothing's been the same since!"

"You used a swear word, Mama!"

Della smiled down at the boy. "I know, Jasper. That's because I'm upset. But don't let me hear you talking like that."

"You won't, Mama. I swear." Jasper grinned at his joke.

Della couldn't help but smile at her son, and Longarm chuckled, too. Galloway was the only one who remained poker-faced.

"I guess somebody needs to fetch the doctor for Hawley. We don't want him to bleed to death in there."

Longarm nodded in agreement. "Yeah. He's got a murder charge to answer to, as well as all his other crimes. I heard him confess that he killed Cullen Johnson, so there shouldn't be any trouble fitting him for the hangman's rope."

Della spoke up. "I'll go. I want to get Jasper home so I

can dry him off and put him to bed, and we'll have to go right past Dr. Chamberlain's office."

"You don't need to be out wandering around the town in the middle of the night by yourself, especially after everything that's happened."

Della shook her head. "I think everything bad that can happen already has, don't you? Besides, you have that man Hawley locked up in there, and . . . and Coolidge and Dennehy are dead, aren't they?"

Galloway shrugged. "That's right. I'm sorry you and the boy had to be here for all this."

"We're safe now, that's all that matters." Della stood up and took Jasper's hand. "Come on, Jasper. We're going to stop at Dr. Chamberlain's house, and then we're going home."

He looked up at her. "No more bad men, Mama?"

She glanced at Galloway, then shook her head. "No, honey. There are no more bad men in Warhorse."

Chapter 16

"That woman's really fond of you."

Longarm waited until after Della and Jasper had left the marshal's office before making the comment. Galloway grimaced and shook his head.

"If she is, she's fond of a lie."

"She thinks she knows you."

"She just thought she did. She was wrong."

Longarm perched a hip on the corner of the desk. He reached into his shirt pocket for one of the three-for-a-nickel cheroots he carried, but of course, all he found was a mass of soggy tobacco. The cheroots were ruined.

"You don't happen to have a smoke around here, do you?"

Galloway gestured toward the desk. "Middle drawer."

Longarm leaned back to open the drawer. He reached inside and brought out a fat cigar. He didn't normally smoke that type, but beggars couldn't be choosers, as the old saying went. He held up the cigar and cocked an eyebrow at Galloway, silently asking if the former outlaw wanted one. Galloway shook his head.

Longarm took a box of matches out of the drawer, too, then used his pocketknife to trim the end of the cigar. He set fire to the gasper and inhaled deeply, then blew a perfect smoke ring. Galloway sat down on the sofa and sighed.

"What are you going to do?"

Longarm shook his head. "About what?"

"Me. You said I was under arrest. You're taking me back to Denver with you?"

Longarm sighed. "I don't have much of a choice, old son. I swore an oath to uphold the law. Now, I've been known to bend that law from time to time, whenever I thought I had to, but I don't reckon this is one of those times."

"Warhorse will be left without anybody to keep the peace."

"We'll stop in Phoenix, and I'll tell the sheriff to be sure and send a deputy up here until the town can find another marshal."

"I'm not asking for any favors, you know. I've done plenty of sorry things in my life. I don't deserve any breaks."

Longarm puffed on the cigar. "Things'll have to play out the way they play out. Like the hymn says, further along we'll know more about it."

A shout came from the cellblock. "Hey! My shoulder's still bleeding back here!"

Galloway stood up and went to the doorway. "We've sent for the doctor. Keep your shirt on, Hawley."

"One of these days . . ." Hawley laughed. "You may have the upper hand now, Ed, but you know it's not going to last. One of these days I'll have you in my sights again, and I won't miss."

"I wish *I* hadn't missed earlier tonight."

"You mean when you ambushed us? Fine, upstanding lawman you are, taking potshots at people on the street, starting gunfights that could've killed who knows how many innocent people."

"Go to hell."

"You keep telling me that, but I'm still here."

Galloway turned away from the cellblock. He went toward the stove, where coffee still simmered in the pot.

Longarm took the cigar out of his mouth. "What did Hawley mean about you ambushing them?"

"Forget it. He just likes to run off at the mouth."

Longarm straightened from his casual stance. "I don't think so. When I came along while you were trading shots with that bunch, *you* started that fight, didn't you?"

Galloway turned his head and stared tight-lipped at Longarm, but he didn't answer the question.

Longarm didn't need him to answer. Hawley's words were enough for him to be able to put it together in his own mind.

"You spotted them as they rode into town. You thought you recognized them, but you weren't sure. So while you were making your rounds, you spied on them and made certain it was your old gang, including Hawley."

"You're telling it." Galloway's voice was flat and hard.

"I reckon you must've panicked a little and lost your head. *You* bushwhacked *them*. Didn't matter you were outnumbered. You just wanted to kill them all before they could expose your secret. You didn't think that through, though."

"I figured if I could get Hawley, the others might give it up. I knew it wasn't likely, but I had to try."

"Almost backfired on you. Probably would have, if I hadn't come along."

Galloway shrugged. "I wasn't thinking straight. All I could think of was how everything I'd worked for over the past two years was in danger."

"And that's why you took a shot at me a little while later."

Galloway gave him a level stare. "All I can say is that I'm sorry, Long. That was before you helped me save Jasper and got us out of that jam in the cellblock. Right then, all I cared about was protecting myself." He paused. "Things have changed now."

"Fair enough." Longarm put the cigar back in his mouth and clamped his teeth down on it. "If I believe you."

"Like you say . . . fair enough."

Longarm smoked in silence for a couple of minutes, then reached for his gun as he heard footsteps outside. He relaxed when he saw Dr. Randall Chamberlain appear in the doorway. The sawbones stopped just outside the door to shake rain from his hat and slicker.

"Mrs. McKittredge told me there was another wounded man here, Marshal. She wouldn't explain what she was doing out so late with her little boy, either." Chamberlain put his hat back on and stepped into the office. "Things seem a bit . . . odd in Warhorse tonight."

Galloway nodded. "That's sure enough true. The man's back in the cellblock."

Chamberlain started in that direction, then stopped short at the sight of the blood and bodies on the floor. "My God!"

"Sorry, Doc. Reckon I should have warned you about that. We, uh, had some trouble a little while ago."

Chamberlain looked back over his shoulder at Galloway. "I should say so."

"Coolidge and Dennehy tried to escape. The fella in the cell is an outlaw they were going to join up with." Galloway shook his head. "It's a long story."

"You can tell me all about it later. Right now I suppose I'd better tend to this man."

Galloway and Longarm exchanged a glance. Longarm knew what the former outlaw meant by the look. If Longarm had his way, Galloway wouldn't be in Warhorse much longer. He'd be on his way back to Denver to stand trial.

Galloway went to the desk and took a Colt out of one of the side drawers. He glanced at Longarm again as if waiting to see if the federal lawman was going to stop him.

Longarm just returned the look impassively. He had a hunch the trouble wasn't over yet, and he was likely to need Galloway's help again. He decided he could trust the former outlaw as long as they were here in Warhorse. Galloway still had a big stake in keeping the town safe.

A stake named Della McKittredge.

"Wait a minute, Doc. I'll unlock the cell for you and stand guard." He glared at Hawley. "This hombre's a tricky son of a bitch."

"Thanks, Marshal." Chamberlain frowned. "I don't recall seeing this man before."

"He just rode in tonight. Name's Noah Hawley."

The key clattered in the lock, and then Galloway swung the door open.

Chamberlain looked over at him. "You know him?"

"I do. Wish I didn't."

Galloway stood guard in the corridor while Dr. Chamberlain removed the crude dressing that either Coolidge or Dennehy had slapped on Hawley's bullet-punctured shoulder. Longarm lounged in the doorway between the cellblock and the office.

Hawley cursed bitterly as Chamberlain cleaned and rebandaged the wound. The medico ignored him and went about the work.

When he was finished, Chamberlain stepped back and nodded. "That ought to hold him. I'll need to check the wound and change that dressing in the morning, Pat. Will that be all right?"

"Yeah, sure, Doc. I'm much obliged."

Chamberlain smiled thinly. "Don't worry. I'll bill the town for my services tonight. And the bill may include a little extra for having to come out in that storm."

"There's one more thing you could do for me, if you don't mind. Can you stop at Barney Schmidt's place?"

Chamberlain nodded and looked meaningfully at the corpses of Coolidge and Dennehy. "Yes, I imagine you'd like to get these fellows out of here. Or what's left of them, anyway."

Chamberlain put his hat and slicker on, then picked up his black medical bag and left the marshal's office.

"I reckon this Barney Schmidt must be the local undertaker? I saw him earlier, but we weren't introduced."

Galloway nodded in reply to Longarm's question. "That's right. Barney's got four strapping sons who help him. They'll carry these bodies out of here."

A few minutes later, more heavy footsteps sounded on the porch. A short, stocky man in a slicker and broad-brimmed hat came in. Spectacles perched on his bulbous nose. He grinned at Galloway.

"I hear you have some more work for me, Marshal."

Galloway waved toward the cellblock. "Right in there, Barney."

Four tall, broad-shouldered, Teutonic-looking young men followed Schmidt into the office. They picked up Coolidge and Dennehy by the legs and shoulders and carried them out of the office. Longarm looked through the open door and saw the undertaker's wagon parked in the street. Schmidt was indeed doing a booming business tonight, and he didn't even know about the two dead outlaws lying between the town and the arroyo. Those bodies could be collected in the morning.

Galloway looked at the bloodstains on the floor and shook his head. "That's gonna be hell to clean up." He grunted. "I suppose it's not my worry, though, is it? I won't be here."

"I might wish things were different, old son, but wishing don't make it so. Anyway, I ain't completely forgotten that you tried to ambush me not more than four hours ago."

"How do you plan on getting me and Hawley back to Phoenix? There are two of us and one of you."

"You're not trying to make me believe that you and him would team up against me, are you?"

Galloway didn't answer for a moment. Then he gave a bitter laugh.

"No, I don't reckon that'll ever happen."

Hawley must have been listening from the cellblock. "It could! I'll split that gold with you, Ed. Just put a bullet in that lawdog's head, and you and me will be partners again."

Galloway stepped to the door into the cellblock and glared

at the prisoner. "Pipe down. The day you and I are partners again, there'll be snow falling in hell."

"Just think about it, that's all I'm saying. All that gold, Ed, and we'd be free men again." Hawley paused. "Of course, you wouldn't have the widow lady, but I don't reckon we can have everything we want in life, can we?"

Galloway turned away from the cellblock. "Just shut up in there, or I'll gag you."

"You're talking like a lawman again, Ed!" Hawley laughed.

Galloway slammed the door between the office and the cellblock. It was a thick wooden panel with a barred window in it. He looked at Longarm.

"You mind?"

"Not one damned bit. Hawley gets annoying in a hurry."

Barney Schmidt and two of his sons came back into the office, water dripping off their hats and slickers. "The bodies are all loaded, Marshal. Anything else we can do for you?"

Galloway shook his head. "Thanks, Barney."

"Oh, you're much obliged, much obliged . . ."

He started to turn away, then stopped and nodded at his sons. The young man leaped at Longarm, each of them grabbing an arm. Longarm barely had time to let out a startled yell before the Schmidt boys slammed him down on top of Galloway's desk.

"What the hell!" The startled exclamation came from Galloway.

"Step aside, Pat." That calm voice belonged to Dr. Randall Chamberlain. As Longarm struggled against the iron grips of his captors, he saw the doctor come into the office and lean over him.

"What are you doing, Doc? Don't—"

"You'll thank us later."

That was the last thing Longarm heard before Chamberlain leaned over him and he smelled ether. A cloth soaked in the stuff came down over his face. Longarm tried not to inhale it, but that was a losing battle. The sickly-sweet smell filled his senses.

Then, for the second time tonight, he went away into darkness.

Chapter 17

When consciousness returned to Longarm this time, his head hurt once again. It was a different kind of pain, though, the result of the drug that Dr. Chamberlain had administered to him, rather than being clouted. This pain made him a little sick at his stomach at first, but the feeling soon went away.

It was replaced by one of confusion. He was lying on his back on something soft, but he realized after a moment that he couldn't move his arms and legs. His eyelids fluttered open. He found himself looking up at the neutral-colored ceiling of a room lit by the soft glow of a lamp that was turned low.

Longarm turned his head first one way, then the other. He saw that ropes were tied securely around each wrist, and then those ropes were tied in turn around the bedposts of the bed where he lay. He didn't go to the trouble of raising his head to try to peer at his feet, because he was reasonably sure they were lashed up the same way.

What the hell . . .?

"You're awake."

The voice that spoke from the doorway was familiar. Longarm jerked his head in that direction and saw Julia

Foster standing there, one shoulder propped casually against the doorjamb, with her arms crossed and an impish smile on her face. Her hair was pulled back and tied with a ribbon behind her head. She looked as pretty as she had earlier in the evening.

Or maybe that was now the previous evening, since the hour had to be getting close to midnight, if it wasn't past that already.

Not that the time mattered all that much, Longarm reminded himself. The important thing was to find out what the hell he was doing here, tied up in Julia's bed.

"Didn't expect to see you again so soon."

"I didn't expect to see you, either. But then when Mr. Schmidt and his sons showed up and said they needed some place to put you tonight, I wasn't going to turn you away."

"Schmidt . . . Was Doc Chamberlain with him?"

Julia nodded. "As a matter of fact, he was. In fact, so was Della McKittredge and Marshal Ryan."

"Did they bother explaining to you that the man you call Ryan is really a train-robbing owlhoot named Galloway?"

Julia came closer to the bed. A solemn expression replaced her smile.

"As a matter of fact, they did. I couldn't believe it at first. After my folks died, Marshal Ryan was so nice to me. Of course, everyone in Warhorse was. But he admitted it was true, and they asked me for my help."

"Doing what?"

"Keeping you out of harm's way."

"Giving them a place to hold me prisoner, you mean."

Julia shrugged. "Call it whatever you want to, Custis. All I know is that the marshal asked for my help, and so did the others. I wasn't going to turn them down."

Longarm recalled that it had been Galloway, still in his pose as Marshal Pat Ryan, who had suggested that he walk Julia home from the café. And it was after he'd left her house that Galloway had tried to ambush him. Galloway hadn't really been worried about Julia; he was just setting Longarm up for that bushwhack attempt.

Galloway would say that things had changed since then, would claim that now he regretted trying to kill Longarm. Longarm wasn't sure he was willing to believe that, though, especially not after this latest double-cross.

But then Longarm recalled that Galloway had acted as surprised as he was when Schmidt's burly sons grabbed him and Dr. Chamberlain came into the office to knock him out with the ether. It seemed likely, or at least possible, that the plan had been cooked up by Chamberlain and Schmidt . . .

And Della McKittredge, thought Longarm. Della was the one who had gone to Chamberlain's house and told him to come to the jail to tend to Noah Hawley's wound. Della was the only citizen of Warhorse who had known the true story of who their marshal really was.

So it had to have been Della who came up with the idea. Despite the anger she had felt toward Galloway earlier for putting Jasper's life in danger, she still had enough feelings for him to want to save him from the fate represented by Longarm.

Those thoughts flashed through Longarm's mind as he looked up at Julia. "Why didn't they just lock me up in the jail? There's an empty cell."

Julia shook her head. "I don't know. Marshal Ryan said he thought you'd be safer here, but he didn't explain why. Maybe he believes that nobody would think to look for you here."

That made no sense at all. Why would Galloway be worried about his safety? And why would he be safer here with this young woman than locked up behind iron bars?

Those answers could wait. Right now he had to talk some sense into Julia's head.

"All right, you need to untie me now."

Julia just stood beside the bed and slowly shook her head from side to side.

"Blast it, Julia, this has gone far enough! Did any of those folks tell you that I'm a deputy United States marshal? Holding me here like this against my will is a federal crime!"

"I'm sorry, Custis. I really am. But these people are my friends. For the past couple of years, they're all the family I have left, too. You can't ask me to turn against them."

"What I'm asking you to do is uphold the law."

"Well . . . that's not really my job, is it? It's yours. And you're a little—"

"Don't say it." Longarm's voice was grim as he issued the warning.

"Tied up at the moment." Julia's smile came back as she ignored him.

"Damnit!"

"Oh, stop complaining, Custis." She sat down beside him on the edge of the bed. "You may not want to be here, but at least you get to spend the night with pleasant company."

As if to illustrate her point, she reached over and rested a soft hand on his crotch, rubbing his cock through his trousers. Longarm didn't want to respond to her touch, but as usual, his manhood had a mind of its own. He felt the shaft starting to stiffen, and so did Julia. She rubbed harder.

"Have you ever been with a woman before like this? When you were tied up, I mean?"

As a matter of fact, he had, although it wasn't exactly his favorite way to experience the pleasures of lovemaking. He wasn't going to tell any of that to Julia, though. He kept his mouth clamped shut and glared at her.

"I found this book once. Some dry-goods drummer accidentally left it behind in the café after he ate there. I ran after him to give it back, but he was already gone and I couldn't find him. So I kept it." She leaned closer to him and lowered her voice. "It was a very naughty book, Custis. It was all about the things that a man and a woman can do together. Some of them I already knew about, but some of them were, well, shocking! That didn't stop me from reading the whole book. Studying it, even."

She moved her hands to his waist and started unfastening his belt buckle.

Good Lord! he thought. He wouldn't have believed there was such a wanton minx under such an innocent-looking exterior.

Unfortunately, that thought just made his cock get even harder.

"There were even drawings in that book, and in one of them, the man was tied to a bed like you are now. The drawings showed all the things a woman could do to him. And of course, there were drawings showing it the other way around, too, and I'd sure like to try *that* sometime, too, but right now you're the one who's tied up and the marshal told me to keep you that way, so I guess we'll just have to settle for that."

She was unbuttoning his trousers by now.

"Blast it, Julia, you don't want to be doing this!"

She laughed. "That's where you're wrong, Custis. I want very much to be doing this." She ran her palm over his erection. "And from the way this feels, so do you."

"A man can't help that—"

"Well, neither can a woman. And that's exactly what I am, because, if you need a reminder, Custis, it was only a few hours ago that you deflowered me."

A groan escaped past his clenched teeth. "Damnit, don't remind me!"

"Oh, Custis, Custis." She leaned over and kissed him as she finished freeing his shaft from his underwear. She wrapped the fingers of one hand as far around the thick pole as they could reach. "We're both going to enjoy this."

Longarm wasn't so sure about that. What with being tied up and all, he thought it was unlikely that he'd enjoy this one little bit. He'd be too busy thinking about how the citizens of Warhorse, instigated by Della McKittredge, had turned on him in defense of the man they regarded as their marshal and friend.

Of course, they were just being loyal . . . and it *did* feel mighty good the way Julia was running her palm up and down the length of his shaft. Like it or not, the flesh throbbed with pleasure under her soft touch.

Longarm bit back the groan that tried to well up his throat as Julia leaned over and wrapped her silky lips around the head of his cock. She spread them wider and engulfed another couple of inches as her hand tightened around the shaft below that. The heat of her mouth seemed to sear Longarm's organ, and as she began to suck gently, it was all he could do to resist the urge to spray his juices down her throat.

Julia continued that exquisite torment for several seconds, then lifted her head and smiled at Longarm. "See? That's not so bad, now is it?"

"It don't matter what you do to me." His voice was hoarse with desire that he couldn't hide. "This is still wrong."

"What we're doing, you mean?"

"You know good and well what I mean. Tying me up this way. Keeping me prisoner so I can't arrest Galloway."

"I don't know anybody named Galloway. The only one I know is Marshal Ryan . . . and I think you're going to find that everybody in Warhorse feels the same way." She hooked her fingers in the waistband of his trousers and started pulling them down. "Let's get these out of the way."

She tugged his trousers down past his knees and followed them with the long underwear. That left his groin exposed with his erection standing straight and tall from it. Julia leaned over again and swirled her tongue around the crown. The heated swipe made Longarm throb again.

She stood up and reached for the hem of her dress. In a simple yet elegant motion, she lifted it, peeled the garment up and over her head. She wore nothing under the dress, so when she tossed it aside, she stood there completely nude, her body glowing golden and beautiful in the soft light from the lamp.

There came a time when a man was a damned fool to go on resisting the inevitable, Longarm told himself. He had already tested his bonds enough to know that they were strong and tight. Whoever had tied him to the bed had known what they were doing when it came to knots.

So if Julia Foster was so hell-bent on having her way with him, he supposed the only thing he could do was let her continue.

She climbed onto the bed with him and moved up until she was straddling his head with a knee on each side of his face. That gave him a mighty fine view of her sweet little honeypot, especially when she reached down, ran her fingers through the silky hair, and spread the pink lips. Despite what she had told him earlier about being enthusiastic and inventive about finding objects she could use to give herself pleasure, her sex was nice and tight, even when she pulled it open like that.

She lowered her hips. "There were drawings in the book of a man licking it. I never would have thought of such a thing myself, but I want to try it. You don't mind, do you, Custis?"

"Would it do any good if I said I did?"

She frowned down at him and looked offended. "Well, for God's sake, it's not like I'm *raping* you or anything. I'd be asking you to do this even if you weren't tied up."

The situation was so ridiculous Longarm suddenly couldn't help but laugh. "Bring it down a little closer, darlin', and I'll see what I can do."

Evidently what he did with his lips and tongue was pretty good, judging by the way Julia commenced to squealing and bouncing around within a few minutes. She grabbed his head and rubbed her juicy core against his face, grinding herself into his mouth as he speared his tongue into her depths. Then he transferred his attention to the little nubbin at the top of her opening and turned those squeals into screams of joy.

Finally, Julia fell limply to the side in what appeared to be utterly satisfied exhaustion. She lay there breathing heavily for several minutes before she recovered. When she had, her hand stole out to caress Longarm's still-erect manhood.

"You made me feel so good, Custis, but you didn't get anything out of it yet. We'll have to do something about that."

Longarm didn't bother asking her what she had in mind. He knew that she'd show him.

He didn't have to wait very long, either. Julia sat up and straddled him again, this time poising herself over his hips. She took hold of his stiff cock and guided it to her opening. Slowly, she let herself slide down onto it, filling herself with him.

Her eyes widened as he penetrated deeper and deeper into her. "Land's sake, Custis, I . . . I thought you filled me up before. This is . . . uh! . . . even better."

She hit bottom at last. He hadn't been sure if she would be able to take all of him into her incredibly tight aperture, but obviously she had been determined to get it all in.

"I don't think . . . I can move." Her voice was a husky whisper. "If I do . . . it's liable to . . . split me right in two. Can I just . . . sit here and enjoy it?"

"I reckon you can do just about anything you want."

She smiled down at him. "I want to feel every inch of you, Custis."

She closed her eyes and sat there smiling with pleasure, impaled on his manhood. But inevitably, her hips began to rock back and forth slightly. That just increased her arousal and made her move even more. Evidently she felt more confident now and wasn't quite as worried about him splitting her in half. Her hips pumped harder. She started to bounce up and down a little.

Longarm wished he could reach up and cup her firm, apple-sized breasts. The hard brown nipples invited his tongue to stroke around them. Not this time, though. Right now, all he could do was struggle to hold back his climax as Julia climbed higher and higher toward the peak.

Suddenly, she spasmed around him, shudders rippling through her body, and Longarm let himself explode. He pumped his juices into her, flooding her already heated interior. She was even wetter and hotter when he was through with her. Her head tipped back, and instead of a scream, this time she let out a long sigh of pure satisfaction.

Then she collapsed on top of him as if she were out cold. For all Longarm knew, she was.

But he could feel her heart hammering against him, so he knew she was all right. She was young and vital, and a good fucking like this was the best thing in the world for her.

Now he could turn his attention to figuring a way to get the hell out of here. The rest of Hawley's gang was still on the other side of the arroyo, and come morning, the citizens of Warhorse would be liable to need his help, whether they wanted it or not.

Chapter 18

When Julia woke up, she was purring again almost immediately and seemed intent on wearing him down to a nub by
morning. Eventually, though, she slept, and so did Longarm.

When he woke up, the window behind the curtains was
still dark. It wasn't dawn yet. But Julia was gone, and he
smelled coffee brewing.

She hadn't pulled his pants up when she left, he noticed.
His pecker was still hanging out for all the world to see, if
all the world ever happened to troop through Julia Foster's
bedroom. Longarm heaved a sigh of exasperation.

She must have heard him. A moment later she appeared
in the doorway, wearing a robe and smiling at him.

"You're awake. I'm working on breakfast. I'm a good
cook, if I do say so myself."

Longarm cocked an ear toward the ceiling. "I don't hear
rain hitting the roof."

"No, it stopped sometime during the night. I guess the
storm has blown over."

She was wrong about that, he thought. The storm might
be just beginning, if those outlaws on the other side of the
arroyo had their way.

One thing about floods in this normally dry country . . . they could go away almost as fast as they showed up. The thirsty flatlands to the east would just drink up all the rain that had fallen the night before. That meant all the water in the arroyo might go away before the morning was over, leaving it clear for Hawley's gang to cross. It would be more difficult with the bridge being washed away, no doubt about that, but certainly not impossible.

Galloway had seemed to think it was impossible that the outlaws could take over the town, and maybe he was right. But innocent people likely would die in the fighting, and Longarm didn't want that if it could be prevented.

The way to avoid that was to stop the fight from ever reaching the streets of Warhorse.

"You need to untie me and let me go now."

Julia frowned. "They told me not to do that."

"The men who brought me here last night?"

"That's right."

"They're just trying to protect Marshal Ryan. But I'm not the only one who's a danger to him. Fact of the matter is, he's got a lot more to worry about than just me, and so does everybody else in Warhorse. There's a gang of outlaws out there that's going to be riding into town later today looking for their boss, and they won't hesitate to gun down anybody who gets in their way."

Julia shook her head. "Nobody said anything about that."

"It's the truth." Longarm made his voice as convincing as possible. That wasn't hard, since he believed what he was telling her. "The whole town's in danger, and I can help stop it."

"I'm sorry." She sounded like she meant it. "Maybe Marshal Ryan will come by later and tell me that I can let you go."

She went back to the kitchen. Longarm muttered some curses, then started looking around for some way he might be able to escape.

The knots around his wrists were tight, and so were the ones around the bedposts. But the posts at the foot of the bed had brass knobs on top of them, and Longarm wasn't sure how those knobs were fastened onto the posts.

If he could work one of them loose . . .

No sooner had the thought crossed his mind than he tried lifting each leg in turn. He wanted to see if he could slide the rope up to the knob and maybe pop it loose somehow.

But with his trousers down around his knees, he couldn't do that. He couldn't lift either leg enough.

"Julia!"

She looked annoyed as she appeared in the doorway again. "I told you I can't turn you loose, Custis. I wish you'd stop asking me to."

Longarm shook his head. "That ain't it. I was just wondering if you could pull my trousers up."

"Why would I do that? I thought we might put that big ol' thing of yours to good use again after breakfast."

Longarm managed not to say *Lord help us*, but he thought it. "We can still do that, but right now . . . well, this is just plumb undignified, Julia."

She had to laugh at that. "All right, if you want to be shy about it . . ." She came over to the bed, gave his cock an affectionate squeeze, then tugged his underwear and trousers back up over his hips. She even fastened the buttons and buckled his belt again. "There. Better?"

"Yep. I'm much obliged."

"Now don't bother me again, or I'll never get breakfast fixed. And you should eat, because you're going to need your strength."

"All right. I'm fine now."

She smiled at him and left the room. Longarm waited until he heard her clattering around in the kitchen again before he went back to what he had tried to do before.

This time he was able to lift his left leg. He forced it as high as he could, and the rope began to slip upward. Longarm worked his leg back and forth, getting all the play in the rope that he could. After what seemed like a long time, he had the rope against the bottom of the brass knob.

He heaved with all the strength he could muster in that leg. At first he thought the knob wasn't going to budge, but then it shifted just slightly. He could tell now that a brass shaft protruded from the bottom of the knob and had been forced down into a hole drilled into the top of the bedpost. That was all that was holding it in place. He took a deep breath and pulled up again with his leg.

The knob acted like it wasn't going to come loose, but when it did, it popped out in a hurry. Longarm's eyes widened as he saw the knob fly up into the air. If it made a racket when it fell, Julia would probably hear it and come rushing in here to see what was going on. If she found him trying to escape, she might run down to the marshal's office for help.

The brass knob seemed to take forever to reach the top of its arc and then come back down. It landed on the mattress between Longarm's spraddled legs and didn't make a sound other than a tiny *plop* that Julia wouldn't be able to hear. Longarm started breathing again.

The rope had slid off the post when the knob came loose. That gave Longarm a little slack. He pushed himself to the right and lifted that leg. Now that he knew it was possible to dislodge the knobs that topped the bedposts, he redoubled his efforts, and as Julia continued to move around in the kitchen and even sing a soft little tune, Longarm worked his other leg free. This time the knob fell on the floor when it came off the post, but luck was with him and Julia clattered some pots and pans at that moment, covering up the sound.

With both legs free, Longarm was able to scoot toward the headboard. He strained to reach the knob on top of the post to his right. The bones and muscles in his arms and shoulders seemed to be stretched almost to the point of cracking, but finally he got his fingers on the knob and began wiggling it back and forth.

The knob rose until the shaft popped out of the hole in the bedpost. Longarm's muscles trembled a little as the strain on them eased. He took the time for a deep breath, then twisted to the left, grabbed the knob on that side with his right hand, and pulled it loose. The ropes were still attached to his wrists and ankles, but he could move around now.

He was swinging his legs off the bed when Julia appeared in the doorway, a tray of food in her hand. The tray slipped from her fingers and crashed to the floor as she saw that he was loose.

"Custis! What—"

Longarm leaped across the room, trailing pieces of rope behind him, and grabbed her as she turned to run. He wrapped his arms around her and hauled her back into the room. She started to struggle, but his grip was tight enough that she had no chance of getting away.

At the same time, he tried to be as gentle about it as he could. Julia wasn't his enemy. She was just trying to help a man she admired and felt grateful to. That was true of Della McKittredge, Dr. Chamberlain, and probably most of the other folks in town, too.

"Settle down, damnit! I'm not going to hurt you."

"Let me go! You shouldn't be loose! When the marshal gets here, he's going to—"

Longarm shifted his grip on her and clamped a hand over her mouth. "Galloway's coming here?"

Julia made angry, muffled noises. Longarm lifted his hand from her mouth, thinking that he was probably lucky she hadn't bit him.

"Of course he's coming here. He said he'd be by around dawn to check on you. That's not far off. Oh!" She twisted her head to try to look at him. "I shouldn't have told you that, should I?"

"I would've guessed it anyway."

Longarm took her over to the bed and put her on it face-down. He straddled her, pinning her to the mattress with his weight. She tried to turn over but couldn't do it.

He worked quickly at the ropes around his wrists with fingers and teeth, loosening the knots until he could slip them off. Then he pulled Julia's arms behind her and lashed her wrists together using one of the pieces of rope.

"I'm mighty sorry about this. The last thing in the world I want to do is hurt you, Julia. I can't afford to have you running around telling folks that I'm loose, though."

"Custis, are . . . are you going to take advantage of me?"

The way he was sitting on her, his groin was pressed against the soft swelling of her rump. She moved it back and forth against him, and he felt himself harden. She must have felt it, too, because despite her anger at him, a husky little moan came from deep in her throat.

"Some other time, darlin'. You've got my word on it. For now, though . . ."

He stood up, rolled her onto her side, and used the other piece of rope to tie her ankles. She couldn't move now.

"I sure hope that ain't too uncomfortable for you. As soon as I can, I'll either turn you loose or see to it that somebody else does."

"Marshal Ryan's going to be so disappointed in me."

"He shouldn't be. I'll tell him it wasn't your fault."

"You're still going to arrest him?"

Longarm thought about how fast the water in that arroyo was probably going down. "Right now I'm going to try to help him stop those owlhoots from raiding the town."

The sound of someone knocking on the front door of Julia's house made Longarm's head turn in that direction. More than likely, that was Galloway coming to check on him as he had promised Julia he would do.

A glance toward the bed told Longarm that Julia was opening her mouth, probably to yell a warning to Galloway that he was free. He leaped across the room and put his hand over her mouth again, muffling her cry.

"Dadgummit, didn't you just hear me say that I want to *help* the marshal?" Longarm used his other hand to pull his bandanna from his shirt pocket. He stuffed it into her mouth, again trying not to be too rough about it. It would only be effective as a gag until she managed to work it out of her mouth, but maybe it would keep her quiet long enough for him to do what needed to be done.

Leaving her on the bed, he hurried into the front room as the knock sounded again on the door. The lamps in this room weren't lit, but enough light came from the kitchen and bedroom for him to be able to find his way around as he catfooted over to the door. He pressed his back against the wall so that when the door opened, it would conceal him for a moment.

Longarm knew that Galloway wouldn't just turn and leave when no one answered his knock. The former outlaw would worry that something was wrong. Sure enough, after a moment, Galloway called out from the porch.

"Julia? Julia, are you in there? It's Marshal Ryan. Open up."

Galloway was still calling himself the marshal of War-horse, Longarm noted. He supposed it was hard to just put that aside after having played the role for two years.

Only Ed Galloway *hadn't* been playing a role, Longarm realized. For all intents and purposes, he had really become Marshal Pat Ryan. He had put his life on the line more than once to protect Warhorse and its citizens. From everything Longarm had heard since arriving here, as well as from the way the townspeople regarded him, Ryan . . . Galloway . . . whoever . . . had been an exemplary peace officer.

Sort it out later, Longarm told himself. Right now there were more pressing problems.

Like the fact that Galloway was opening the door next to Longarm. He stepped into the house, and as he moved past the door, Longarm saw the gun in his hand.

"Julia?"

A heavy thump came from the bedroom. Julia must have rolled off the bed. Longarm hadn't had time to tie her securely enough to prevent that.

The noise was enough to alarm Galloway. He took a quick step toward the bedroom, the gun in his hand coming up as he did so.

Longarm made his move.

Chapter 19

Longarm's left arm looped around Galloway's neck while he used the edge of his right hand to chop down on the wrist of the man's gun hand. Galloway yelled in surprise, a reaction that was cut off short as Longarm's arm clamped down on his throat. The blow to the wrist made the gun slip from Galloway's fingers. It thudded to the floor, and Longarm counted himself lucky that the impact didn't make it go off.

He gave Galloway a shove that sent the man stumbling across the room. With a swift move, Longarm scooped up the revolver and leveled it as Galloway caught his balance and started to whirl around toward him.

"Hold it, Galloway!"

"How the hell did you get loose?" Galloway's voice was harsh with anger. "Damn you, Long, if you hurt that girl—"

"Take it easy. Julia's fine." Other than being a mite loco on the subject of fooling around, Longarm thought. "I wouldn't hurt her. She's in the bedroom."

Longarm motioned with the gun for Galloway to go in there. He wanted to make sure Julia hadn't hurt herself when she rolled off the bed.

She appeared to be fine, just mad as a wet hen as she glared up from the floor at Longarm. She had almost managed to push the bandanna out of her mouth with her tongue, and she succeeded as Longarm and Galloway came into the room.

"You . . . you big old . . . *bully*!"

Longarm had to smile. "I reckon I've been called worse. Galloway, help the little lady up. Julia, just sit on the edge of the bed and take it easy for a few minutes while the marshal and I talk."

Galloway helped Julia to her feet and glanced at Longarm in surprise as he did so. "Marshal?"

Longarm shrugged. "That's how the folks in this town see you, and I reckon I'm outnumbered right now. For the time being, we need to be working together, not fighting."

"Against the rest of Hawley's bunch, you mean."

Longarm nodded. "That's right."

"I'm going to handle them. The townspeople will help me. Doc Chamberlain, Barney Schmidt and his sons, Davidson over at the café . . . they've all said they'll pitch in. I reckon some of the other citizens will, too."

"I don't doubt it, but how many of those folks are professional fighting men?"

"Well . . . none of 'em. You know that. But they're tough and brave and willing to fight."

"And some of them will get killed." Longarm's voice was flat and hard. "*You* know *that*."

Galloway grimaced. "Yeah, you're probably right. But what do you suggest?"

Longarm took a chance and reversed the Colt in his hand so that it was butt-forward. He held out the weapon to Galloway.

"That the two of us stop them before they get to the settlement. Folks here need to be warned and ready in case that wild bunch gets past us, but you and I will try to keep them from ever getting here."

Galloway hesitated, then reached out and took the gun from Longarm. From the look on his face, he wasn't sure for a second what he wanted to do with it.

But then he slipped it back into the holster on his hip. "How do we do that?"

"What's the best place for them to cross the arroyo? I'm betting it's not right there where the bridge was."

Galloway shook his head. "No, the bridge was built there because the banks were good and firm and level on both sides. The banks are too steep to climb, though, almost sheer, in fact. But there's a place about a quarter of a mile up where the slope is a lot easier because the banks partially caved in sometime in the past. You have to lead horses to get them up and down there, but it can be done."

Longarm nodded. "Sounds like just the place they'd pick to cross. Is there any good cover around it?"

Julia spoke up before Galloway could answer. "If you two are just going to stand around making plans, don't you think that somebody could untie me first?"

Longarm chuckled. "You promise to behave yourself?"

She glared at him, and for a second he thought she might tell Galloway all about how the two of them had been behaving for a good part of the night. True, the romping had been more her idea than Longarm's, but Galloway might not see it that way.

"All right, all right, hang on." Longarm moved to the side of the bed and bent over to reach behind Julia and untie the rope around her wrist. He hadn't tied it very tightly to begin with. She could have worked her way loose without much trouble.

While he was doing that, Galloway answered the question Longarm had asked a moment earlier. "There are some trees and a little cluster of rocks not far from that spot we were talking about. Are you thinking about forting up there and ambushing those boys when they come out of the arroyo?"

"That's exactly what I was thinking."

Galloway rubbed his jaw and frowned in thought. "That wouldn't be too fair, throwing down on them without any warning like that."

"It wouldn't be fair to let them kill any number of innocent people in town trying to get to Hawley, either."

"Yeah, but I rode with some of those men. I could always just let Hawley go. Maybe he'd take the gold and move on."

"You really think so?"

Galloway didn't have to ponder that question for very long. After a couple of heartbeats, he shook his head.

"Hawley would think that was the perfect opportunity to loot the town. There would still be killing."

"That's what I thought. Stopping them before they get here is our best bet."

"You're right." Galloway sighed. "I don't have to like it, though."

"Lawmen have to do a lot of things they don't really like."

Galloway glanced toward the window. "We'd better get moving if we're going to get in position in those trees without them seeing us. It's already getting light."

That was true. Longarm could see a faint gray glow beyond the curtains. As he left Julia's house with Galloway, he saw that the sky was still thickly overcast with dark clouds, which helped matters. The gloom would come in handy.

Behind them, Julia stepped into the doorway. "Marshal, is there anything I can do?"

Both men stopped to look back, instinctively responding to the word "marshal." Galloway was the one who answered her.

"Stay home and keep your door locked. If Marshal Long and I don't stop those varmints, they'll be heading here for town."

Julia paled and nodded and went back inside. Longarm and Galloway hurried toward the marshal's office and jail.

The streets were still a quagmire, but at least no rain was falling at the moment. Longarm cast an eye toward the thick gray clouds overhead.

"Reckon the storm's over?"

"I don't know. I hope so. This is already the worst storm I've seen in the two years I've been here. It's probably been a long time since they've gotten this much rain around here."

"Been pretty dry lately, has it?"

"It usually is."

"That means the ground will soak up the moisture and the water in the arroyo will go down that much faster."

Galloway wore a grim expression as he nodded. "That's right. We've got an hour, maybe, before it'll be low enough for the rest of the gang to cross it. It'll take them a little while to find that place, too."

"What if they try to cross somewhere else?"

Galloway shook his head. "They won't. That's the best spot. Damn near the only spot where you can get horses up and down the bank."

Hearing that made Longarm feel a little better. He and Galloway still faced a hard fight, but at least they would have a chance to stop the gang from reaching town.

After a long, hard night, Warhorse appeared to still be asleep this morning, at least for the most part. Lamplight glowed in a few windows, but not many. No one was out slogging through the mud except Longarm and Galloway.

They reached the marshal's office and went inside. Their heavy footsteps must have roused Hawley from sleep. Longarm heard the cell door rattle as the outlaw grabbed the bars and shook it.

"Hey! Hey, Ed! What are you doing out there? Trying to figure out how long it'll be before the rest of the boys come into town and fill you full of lead?"

Galloway stepped into the doorway between the office and the cellblock. "That wouldn't be very smart. You don't know for sure that I told you the truth about where that gold is cached."

Hawley laughed. "Yes, I do. I saw the look on your face when I told you what was about to happen to that pretty little widow. You would've sold your soul right then to protect her, let alone a mess of gold."

"Think whatever you want, you son of a bitch." Galloway turned away from the cellblock and closed the door.

He couldn't close out the sound of Hawley's jeering laughter, though.

Longarm knew Hawley was right. Galloway had told them the true location of that gold cache. But the knowledge wouldn't do Hawley any good unless his men succeeded in freeing him.

Right now, the rest of the outlaws didn't know where Hawley was or even that he was still alive. They couldn't, because they had been on the other side of the arroyo ever since the bridge washed out. All they knew was that Hawley and two members of the gang had reached this side and gone after Galloway.

If they made it to town, though, it wouldn't take them long to find out where their leader was. Warhorse wasn't that big a place. And they would kill anybody who got in their way.

Galloway went to the gun cabinet. "Better load up."

Longarm couldn't have agreed more with that sentiment. He didn't know where his gun belt was, but he tucked two Colts behind his regular belt, took a Winchester from the rack, and filled his pockets with .44-40 cartridges that would fire in either weapon. Galloway did likewise, arming himself with all the guns and ammunition he could carry.

When they were ready, Galloway led the way from the marshal's office toward the northern edge of town. Warhorse Mountain loomed blackly over the settlement. The gray of the peak blended with the gray of the overcast sky so that it was difficult to tell where one ended and the other began. To the east, though, there were a few red streaks in the gray that told Longarm the clouds were trying to break up. By midday, the sun would probably be out, baking the moisture out of the muddy ground and turning it back into hard-packed earth.

Galloway cut through an alley and brought them out at the rear of several buildings. Using those buildings to shield them from the view of any of the outlaws who might spot them through the murk, they worked their way out of town and then ran toward the arroyo, aiming for a spot well north of the bridge. The sky began to lighten even more as they neared the trees and rocks Galloway had mentioned.

A moment later, they reached cover and stopped to catch their breaths.

"I'm glad we didn't wait any longer." Galloway pointed. "I think they're on the move."

Longarm looked the way the former outlaw was pointing and saw movement in the gloom. After a moment, the shadowy shapes took on more definition. Longarm recognized them as the members of the gang who had been left on the far side of the arroyo. He tried to count them but was unsure whether there were eight or nine.

Either way, it wasn't very good odds.

But he and Galloway would have the element of surprise on their side, Longarm reminded himself, plus they had some decent cover while the outlaws would be out in the open. It would all come down to how quickly they could drop some of the owlhoots. If their shots were effective as soon as they opened fire, they might have a chance to whittle the odds down to something less overpowering.

Longarm went to one knee behind a rock at the edge of the trees, ignoring the fact that the knee of his trousers immediately turned wet and muddy. He had been soaked and covered with mud so many times in the past twelve hours he wasn't sure he would ever be clean and dry again. Right now, he didn't care.

"See where the ground dips a little, right there at the edge of the arroyo?" Galloway knelt beside him and pointed. "That's where they'll come up. They'll be leading their horses. We need to get as many of 'em as we can, as fast as we can."

"Even the ones you used to ride with?" Longarm wanted to be sure he could count on Galloway. That was why he asked the question.

"Even them." The answer was flat and hard. "They chose their trail, and I chose mine. If they've been riding with a murdering skunk like Hawley for two years, they're not the men I knew anymore."

"All right. Looks like they're starting down into the arroyo. Shouldn't be long now, as the saloon girl said to the preacher."

They watched as the outlaws dismounted on the far side of the arroyo and one by one led their mounts down the partially caved-in bank. Longarm counted them again and got a total of nine. A little over four to one odds. He had faced worse and come out on top, but sooner or later his luck had to run out.

Not today, he hoped. For the sake of the citizens of Warhorse, not today.

Galloway's voice was soft, even though they were about fifty yards from the arroyo and not likely to be overheard. "Let all of them get out of the wash. I'm hoping they'll wait until they're all out to mount up, but if any of them are already on horseback, take them down first, then go for the others."

"That's the way I figured to do it."

Galloway smiled. "They say great minds work alike. I'm gonna move over that way a little so we won't be bunched up. Wait for my shot, then open up on them."

Galloway had turned into a lawman, all right, thought

Longarm. At least, he was giving orders like one. Longarm didn't bother arguing with him. Galloway was a top-notch fighting man. He was going about this the same way Longarm would have.

The former outlaw positioned himself behind a tree about fifty feet from Longarm. They waited. The sound of voices came to Longarm's ears, followed by hoofbeats made dull by the mud. The crown of a man's hat came into view, followed by the rest of it and the man himself, along with the horse he was leading.

The outlaws emerged from the arroyo, gathering in a clump not far from the edge of the wash. The first ones to come out were talking among themselves and made no move to swing up into their saddles. Longarm settled the Winchester's sights on one of them, a round-faced hombre with a walrus mustache. As Longarm peered over the rifle's barrel at the outlaw, he suddenly felt moisture strike his cheek.

It was starting to rain again.

Galloway's gun cracked like a bolt of lightning, and Longarm forgot about the rain. He pulled the trigger, felt the Winchester buck against his shoulder as it fired.

The fight was on.

Chapter 20

Walrus mustache went down. Longarm had aimed for the biggest target, the man's barrel chest. The outlaw hadn't even hit the ground before Longarm had levered another round into the rifle's firing chamber and shifted his aim.

His next target was a skinny gent in a flat-crowned hat and a long frock coat. The man was looking around wildly, trying to locate the source of the shots, when the slug from Longarm's rifle tore through his body, driving him back against his mount. All the horses were starting to move around nervously, spooked by the shots. When the wounded animal bumped heavily into his mount, the animal reared up and lashed out with its hooves. One of the steel-shod feet landed in the middle of the wounded man's face and turned it into a crimson ruin.

That was two down, thought Longarm . . . no, three, because one of the men Galloway had targeted had fallen, too . . . and Longarm and Galloway were both still spraying lead into the group as fast as they work the levers on their rifles.

The outlaws had spotted the muzzle flashes from the trees and the rocks by now, though, and several of them clawed guns from holsters and started returning the fire. At this range, the Winchesters wielded by Longarm and Galloway were more accurate, but Hawley's men weren't worried all that much about aiming. They just pointed their Colts toward the trees and started blazing away.

Longarm had to duck down behind the rock as several bullets whipped past his head close enough for him to hear the wind-rip of their passage. Another couple of slugs ricocheted off the boulder with high-pitched whines.

Off to Longarm's left, the fierce volley from the outlaws had forced Galloway to retreat behind the tree trunk. Bark and splinters flew in the early morning air as lead chewed into wood.

Pounding hoofbeats prompted Longarm to risk another look at the enemy. Three of the outlaws had made it into their saddles, and now they were charging toward the trees, still firing as they rode hard toward the two lawmen.

The continuing barrage from the three owlhoots still on foot made it difficult for Longarm and Galloway to do anything about the ones galloping toward them. If they didn't stop that charge, though, the outlaws would be right on top of them in a matter of moments.

Longarm risked sticking his head up above the rock. A bullet sizzled past his ear. He brought the Winchester to his shoulder, drew a bead on an outlaw's chest, and squeezed off a shot. The slug hit the tag dangling on a string from the tobacco pouch in the man's shirt pocket and plowed right on through into his chest. The outlaw went backward out of the saddle as if he'd been swatted by a giant fist.

At the same time, though, Galloway yelled in pain, dropped his rifle, and staggered out from behind the tree where he had taken cover. Longarm glanced that direction and saw blood on the sleeve of Galloway's shirt. The wound didn't look too bad.

What was bad was that Galloway was out in the open now. He had to dive belly-down onto the ground in order to avoid the bullets that whistled through the space where he had been a heartbeat earlier.

Longarm didn't have time to worry about Galloway. He shifted his aim to another of the mounted outlaws as a bullet spanged off the rock right in front of him, throwing rock dust in his eyes. That made him squint as he pulled the trigger and must have thrown off his aim, because the outlaw closest to him kept coming. The man swung his gun toward Longarm, who tried to lever another round into the Winchester's firing chamber even as he saw flame belch from the muzzle of the owlhoot's Colt.

He expected to feel the shock of a bullet. Instead, he saw the outlaw tumble out of his saddle. From Galloway's position on the ground, the former outlaw had drawn one of his pistols and fired up at an angle, shading the man's shot by a whisker.

That had saved Longarm's life but left Galloway at the mercy of the third rider, who was about to trample him. Longarm snapped a shot with the Winchester, aiming at horse instead of rider this time. The outlaw's mount screamed as its front legs folded up underneath it just a few yards short of where Galloway lay. The violent collapse pitched the rider out of the saddle and sent him sailing through the air.

The outlaw landed hard and rolled over a couple of times. Galloway's gun was roaring in his fist before the outlaw even came to a stop. The man's body jerked under the impact of the slugs, and when he stopped rolling, he lay still as blood welled from his wounds.

That left the three men still at the arroyo, whose guns had fallen mysteriously silent.

That was because they weren't *at* the arroyo anymore, Longarm realized when he looked in that direction. The attack by their compadres had given the other three men enough time to leap into the saddles and take off.

Instead of galloping toward Longarm and Galloway, the remaining trio of outlaws was circling around the trees and rocks and heading straight for the settlement.

"Damnit!" Galloway struggled onto his knees. "We've got to stop them!"

Longarm shared that sentiment, but the three shots he threw after the hard-riding owlhoots didn't find their marks. The outlaws vanished into the gloom that had thickened since the light rain began falling.

He knew the men must have decided to abandon their companions and try to make it into town so they could look for Hawley. Even though Longarm and Galloway had stopped the whole gang from descending on Warhorse, the three who had gotten away were more than enough to kill some innocent people in the settlement.

Longarm ran over to Galloway, grabbed his uninjured arm, and helped him to his feet. "How bad are you hit?"

"Nothing to worry about. Bullet went straight through and missed the bone. It hurt like hell and it'll bleed some, but it's not gonna kill me."

"Let's see if we can catch a couple of those horses and get after those sons of bitches, then."

The horses belonging to the dead outlaws were spooked because the shooting and the smells of blood and powder smoke that hung in the air. Longarm thought that the rain should have scrubbed those smells away, but they lingered stubbornly. Or maybe he just thought they did because he had smelled them so many times in his life.

After a few minutes, they were able to catch two of the horses and swing up into the saddles. Then they headed for Warhorse at a hard gallop.

Even before they got there, they heard shots ring out. Galloway cast an angry, frightened glance at Longarm and leaned forward, urging his commandeered mount on to greater speed. Longarm did likewise. The thing they had tried so hard to prevent was taking place up there ahead of them. Innocent folks were in danger. Maybe Della McKittredge, maybe her boy Jasper, maybe Doc Chamberlain or Julia Foster or big, bluff Arnie Davidson from the Red Top Café. It didn't matter who. Lawlessness had come galloping into Warhorse this morning, and that simple fact got Longarm's dander up.

The hooves of the horses they were riding slid some in the mud as they rounded a corner into Main Street. The hour was still early enough that not many people would be out and about yet, especially since the rain had started again.

The street was deserted right now, though, except for a man crawling through the mud toward an alley. Longarm recognized him as one of Barney Schmidt's sons. The undertaker's boy was dragging a bloody leg behind him.

Shots blasted from the open door of the marshal's office as Longarm and Galloway headed toward the wounded man. The bullets whistled past their heads as they flung themselves out of the saddle and each of them grabbed one of the Schmidt boy's arms.

"Over here!"

The shout came from the alley toward which the youngster had been heading. Longarm spotted Dr. Randall Chamberlain standing just inside the mouth of the passageway with a gun in his hand. He and Galloway half carried, half dragged the wounded man into the shelter of the alley.

"What happened, Doc?" Galloway's voice was tense as he asked the question. He and Longarm lowered the Schmidt youngster so that he was sitting on the ground with his back propped against the wall of the building next to them.

"Several of us were standing guard, just as we discussed last night, Pat. Julia told us that you and Marshal Long were going to try to stop Hawley's men as they crossed the arroyo, but we wanted to be ready in case you weren't able to."

"We tried." Galloway's tone was bitter now. "We got six of them, but three got past us."

Chamberlain nodded. "I know. I can see that you're hit, too. Maybe I should—"

Galloway interrupted the sawbones with a shake of his head. "Don't worry about me, I'll be fine. What happened when those bastards got here?"

"We opened fire on them, but they were too fast for us. They made it to the jail and started firing back along the street. Gunther here got caught out in the open and wounded. They've been able to keep us pinned down ever since. No one even dared step out to go and try to help him, until you and the marshal came along."

"Where is everybody?"

"Scattered along the street, inside buildings, on top of them, in alleys." Chamberlain rapidly pointed out the positions of Barney Schmidt and his other three sons, Josh Willard, and a couple of other townsmen Longarm hadn't met.

"What about Davidson?"

Chamberlain grimaced and shook his head. "He was in the jail, watching over the prisoner. There were some gunshots in there when those outlaws broke in . . ."

Galloway muttered a curse.

"It's even worse than that, Pat." Chamberlain's face was bleak now. "Julia was in there, too. She had just brought some food over from the café for Arnie."

Longarm stiffened as a finger of ice ran along his spine. His hand tightened around the butt of the Colt he had drawn from behind his belt. He took a step toward the street.

Galloway stopped him with a firm hand on his arm. "You step out there and they'll cut you down, Long."

"How about if we make a try for the back door, then? We have to get in there before they hurt Julia."

Chamberlain spoke up again. "I was in there earlier myself, and Arnie had the back door barred. Those men wouldn't have been foolish enough to unbar it. Their horses are still out front."

"How did they know Hawley was locked up?"

"They grabbed the old man who works part-time as a hostler for Willard and made him talk. Beat him half to death in the process. Willard wasn't at the stable when it happened, but he found the old-timer a couple of minutes later."

Galloway took a deep breath. "All right, they're in there, and by now they've turned Hawley loose. Staying in there won't do them any good. It won't put them a step closer to that gold, and that's what this is all about."

"What about vengeance on you for double-crossing them?"

"I told you before, Marshal, vengeance doesn't mean a damned thing to that bunch without the gold to go along with it. They won't stay holed up in there once they find out that I told Hawley where the gold is hidden."

Chamberlain glanced toward Galloway, and Longarm thought he knew what the sawbones was thinking. The citizens of Warhorse were still having a hard time believing that their lawman was really a train robber, even though they had no choice but to do so. They had heard Galloway's own words confirm it.

"They'll be coming out." Galloway nodded as he spoke, as if it were inevitable. "And they'll have at least one hostage with them."

The shooting had stopped once Longarm and Galloway reached the safety of the alley, and an eerie silence had hung over the street ever since. Now that silence was broken by a shout from the marshal's office.

"I know you're down there, Ed! You'd damned well better listen to me!"

Longarm recognized Noah Hawley's arrogant tones. So did Galloway. He stepped to the corner so that he could call back to Hawley without exposing himself to gunfire.

"I hear you, Hawley! What do you want?"

"Listen to this!"

A woman's scream ripped through the damp air. It had stopped raining again, but an oppressive heaviness gripped the town like the storm might explode again at any second.

Longarm felt a stab of fury at that scream. He could tell by the sound of it that it was motivated more by fear than by pain, so he hoped that Julia was still all right, at least relatively speaking.

"You hear that, Ed?"

"I hear it! Let that girl go, damnit!"

Hawley's mocking laughter rang along the street. "I don't think so. She's our ticket out of here. More than that, she's our ticket to that gold! You're gonna let us go get it, Ed, and then ride away from here without bothering us."

"I don't give a damn about the gold! Just let Julia go, and you can do whatever you want!"

"You fucking this one just like you've been fucking the widow, Ed? I don't believe that. Just like I don't believe that you'd really let us go if we didn't have a hostage! She's coming with us! We'll let her loose once we're away from here!"

Galloway blew out his breath between clenched teeth. "He's lying. He'll kill Julia."

Longarm nodded. "More than likely. And you were lying, too. You weren't going to let him get away if he turned her loose."

"Hell, no! But I figured he wouldn't be that stupid, and he wasn't. So now we've got a standoff again."

"We don't stand a chance of saving Julia as long as they're inside the jail. We've got to get them out of there so we'll have room to operate." Longarm looked steadily at

Galloway. "We've got to give Hawley what he wants . . . for now."

"Let him go after the gold, you mean."

"That's right." Longarm took a deep breath. "But I'm going to be there waiting for him."

Chapter 21

Galloway agreed to stall Hawley as long as he could, to allow Longarm time to get in position. Quickly, he gave the big lawman detailed directions for how to find the place where the stolen gold was hidden.

Dr. Chamberlain straightened from his task of patching up Gunther Schmidt's wounded leg. The young man would be hobbling around for a while, but he ought to be all right, Chamberlain declared.

Then the doctor looked at Longarm. "And I'm going with you."

A frown creased Longarm's forehead. "I ain't sure that's a good idea, Doc."

"You'll be one man against four if you go up there by yourself." Chamberlain hefted the rifle he had leaned against the building wall. "I can use this, you know. I'm an excellent shot, if I do say so myself."

Longarm looked at Galloway, who shrugged. "Might give you a better chance of getting Julia away from them safely."

Longarm reached a decision. "All right, Doc. You can come with me. But I'll be in charge, up there on the mountain."

"I wouldn't have it any other way, Marshal, I assure you."

Hawley's voice came from the jail again. He sounded like he was getting impatient.

"Don't you ignore me, Ed! You owe me some respect, after the way you double-crossed me and the other boys!"

Galloway went back to the corner of the building. "Hold your horses! I'm thinking about how we're going to do this."

"I'll tell you how we're going to do this! You're going to bring me a horse and enough packhorses to tote those bags of gold, too!"

Longarm nodded to Galloway and spoke quietly. "Work out the details with him, and take your time about it. The doc and I will be on that bench where those pine trees are when Hawley and his boys start up the canyon."

Galloway nodded and raised a hand in farewell. "Good luck."

Longarm and Chamberlain trotted along the alley, carrying their rifles. They heard Galloway carrying on the shouted negotiations with Hawley behind them, but the sounds soon faded as rain began pounding down again.

"If I didn't know better, I'd say that we needed to start building a big boat."

Despite the grimness of the situation, Longarm had to grin over at the doctor. "This is Warhorse Mountain we're fixing to climb, Doc, not Ararat. It'll stop raining sooner or later."

"I don't think I'll ever be dry again. I believe I'm actually beginning to grow some gills."

Longarm realized that Chamberlain was making jokes because he was scared. Doctors faced life-and-death situations quite often, but they usually didn't involve gunplay that the doctors themselves were mixed up in.

"You know, Doc, for a little while last night, I actually wondered if you might be Ed Galloway."

"Me?" Chamberlain was visibly surprised. "You thought I was the outlaw you came to Warhorse to find?"

"Well, you match Galloway's description, sort of. About as well as Marshal Ryan does, to tell the truth. And you've been here two years, too, like him. It could have been you."

"I almost wish it was." Chamberlain sighed. "I think Warhorse could better afford to lose me than Pat Ryan. He's a good man, Marshal. He doesn't deserve to go to prison. He didn't kill anyone."

"He robbed a bunch of trains, though, before he partnered up with Hawley and things went wrong for him. You saying he shouldn't have to pay for that, Doc?"

"I don't know what I'm saying. I believe in justice, but . . ."

They were at the foot of the mountain now. "Better save your breath, Doc. We'll need it for climbing. That slope is pretty steep."

That was certainly true. A man on horseback could make it in dry weather, but Longarm wasn't sure that was possible now. The trail leading up the mountain was well defined enough that he had no trouble following it, but it was also slick from the rain. The two men had to be careful. They slipped several times and went to a knee in the mud.

"How's Hawley going to get packhorses up here for the gold?"

"It won't be easy. They'll have to leave their saddle mounts here and lead the packhorses up and then back down." Longarm paused and turned his head to look down at Warhorse. He could barely make out the outlines of the buildings, and they were blurred because of the rain.

That was good. It meant that if Hawley and the other outlaws had started in this direction, they wouldn't be able to see Longarm and Chamberlain climbing Warhorse Mountain ahead of them.

The going was slow and arduous, but eventually Longarm spotted the narrow canyon branching off from the trail.

It looked like someone had carved a gash in the side of the mountain with a giant knife. He tapped Chamberlain on the shoulder and then pointed, and the doctor nodded in agreement. That was their destination.

The canyon floor wasn't quite as steep as the trail they had been following. They were able to make better time without slipping and sliding as much. After another quarter hour, Longarm spotted the ledge that jutted out from the canyon wall on the left side. It had the two pine trees on it that Galloway had mentioned. A narrow trail led up to the ledge.

Beyond it, Longarm could see where the canyon wall jutted out to form the overhang Galloway had talked about as well. The bags of gold bars were hidden in the cavelike area under that overhang. That is, they were if Galloway had been telling the truth, and like Hawley, Longarm was convinced that he had been.

Longarm pointed out the ledge and the overhang to Chamberlain. They started up the trail toward the ledge.

When they reached it, Longarm knelt behind one of the trees, the doctor behind the other. Chamberlain cleared his throat nervously.

"What are we going to do when they get here, Marshal?"

"They'll be leading those packhorses and then loading the gold, so chances are they won't be paying as much attention to Julia. We'll wait for a time when she's clear, then open fire on the varmints and hope she runs back the other way. With any luck, we'll down the four of them before they know what's going on."

"Kill them in cold blood, you mean."

Longarm heard the disapproval in the doctor's voice and saw it on his lean face. "I know that goes against the grain for a man whose business is saving lives, Doc, but it can't be helped. If we give them a chance to surrender, that'll just put Julia's life in even more danger, because they won't do it. They'll put up a fight, and there's a good chance Hawley or one of the others will grab Julia and try to use her as a human shield. That ain't what we want."

Slowly, Chamberlain shook his head. "You're right, Marshal. That's not what we want. I know that. It's just . . . difficult . . . to accept the fact of what has to be done here."

"I know, Doc. I'd be surprised if it *wasn't* hard for you."

They fell silent again and waited as the rain came down on them. Longarm had hoped that he would be able to hear the hoofbeats of the packhorses as the outlaws led them up the canyon, but with the rain making so much noise, that was going to be difficult. Thunder rumbled so loudly that Longarm felt the ground vibrate a little under his feet.

He had to rely on sight rather than sound, and after what seemed like an eternity but was probably more like a half hour, he spotted movement in the canyon. He waited a moment for the shapes to resolve themselves in the rain, then reached over and tapped Chamberlain on the shoulder.

"Here they come, Doc."

Chamberlain stiffened and swallowed hard. "I'm ready."

Longarm hoped that was really true.

He watched as the group of men and horses came closer, and a grimace pulled at his mouth as he saw how they were arranged. The three surviving members of Hawley's gang came first, each man leading a packhorse. Then came Ed Galloway with his hands tied together in front of him. His shirt sleeve was bloody from the wound he had suffered earlier. Hawley brought up the rear with Julia, his wounded left arm around her waist, a gun in his right hand. From the looks of it, he didn't intend to let her go, and Longarm remembered that Hawley was a smart son of a bitch. He was probably afraid of some sort of trick—rightly so, of course—and knew that keeping Julia close to him gave him the best chance of staying alive.

"What are we going to do?" The question came from Dr. Chamberlain in a strained whisper.

"Just wait a spell. We'll see how the hand plays out."

Longarm knew they couldn't open fire, though, not as long as Hawley had Julia at his side and a gun in his hand. The boss outlaw stopped almost directly under the ledge with Julia and Galloway while the other three men went on to drag the bags of gold out from under the overhang.

Galloway's presence came as no surprise to Longarm. He had expected that Hawley would insist on bringing his former partner along. Getting the gold might be paramount, but Hawley still wanted revenge on Galloway, too. Once the loot was loaded on the packhorses, Longarm had no doubt that Hawley planned to kill Galloway or at least have his men do it. They would probably enjoy filling the man who had double-crossed them with lead.

The men with the packhorses stopped. One man took the reins of all three animals, while the other two outlaws bent to look into the narrow space under the brooding overhang of rock.

"I can't see anything, Noah! I don't know if the bags are in there or not!"

"Well, strike a match so you can see, damnit!" Hawley sounded impatient.

"Our matches are all wet. They ain't gonna light."

Galloway spoke up. "The gold's there. If they'll just reach in and feel around, they'll find it."

"You heard the man. Get to work."

The two outlaws crouched in front of the opening looked at each other and shrugged. They leaned forward, and each man shoved an arm up under the rock.

Then they screamed and lurched back, and Longarm's eyes widened as he saw the fat rattlesnakes, two of them attached to each outlaw's hand by deep-driven fangs.

"You son of a bitch!" The furious shout came from Hawley as he jerked his gun up and pointed it at Galloway, who spun around and lurched toward him.

"Run, Julia!"

Hawley's gun belched smoke and flame, and Longarm knew the outlaw couldn't have missed at that range. But even though Galloway was hit, his momentum carried him forward so that he crashed into Hawley and knocked him away from Julia.

At the same time, Longarm came up out of his crouch and lined his Winchester's sights on the man holding the reins of the packhorses. The hombre was clawing at his holstered gun with his other hand. As the man's iron slid out of leather, Longarm squeezed the trigger. The rifle cracked and sent a .44-40 slug smashing into the outlaw's forehead. It bored on through his brain and exploded out the back of his skull with a spray of blood and bone that splattered across the rump of one of the horses. The pouring rain washed it away quickly.

A head shot was always a tricky thing, but Longarm had risked it because it was also the best way to insure that a man didn't have a chance to get a shot off. The outlaw dropped like a rock, dead before he hit the ground.

Thunder crashed, shaking the mountain again as Long arm swung his rifle toward the other two owlhoots. They were still flailing and thrashing around as they tried to dislodge the snakes that had bitten them. They didn't give a damn about anything else at the moment, and with that much venom coursing through their veins, Longarm figured they'd be dead within minutes.

"My God." Chamberlain sounded shocked beyond belief by what he was seeing.

Julia's screams made Longarm whirl in that direction again. He saw Galloway and Hawley rolling around on the muddy ground, engaged in a desperate, life-and-death struggle. Galloway was handicapped by his wound and by having his hands tied, but he had managed to get hold of the wrist of Hawley's gun hand and kept the revolver's barrel shoved away from him.

Hawley was wounded, too, but bad shoulder or not, he

hammered that fist into Galloway's face, hitting him again and again as Julia stood nearby, crying out for help. Longarm lifted the rifle and tried to draw a bead on Hawley, but he realized he couldn't risk the shot, not with Galloway so close.

Another deafening rumble of thunder sounded, but then Longarm's head jerked up as he realized the sound wasn't thunder at all. He looked above him at the wall of the canyon and saw a huge mass of mud and rock sliding toward them. The rain must have loosened something up there, and the shaking from the thunder had finished the job of starting the slide.

And now everyone down here in the canyon was in the path of that deadly avalanche.

Chapter 22

Longarm grabbed Chamberlain's arm and jerked the medico to his feet. "Come on, Doc! We gotta get out of here!"

They ran to the trail and started bounding down it. There was no time to be careful now. The rockslide was moving slowly at the moment, but it would gather steam as it continued to build and start to move faster and faster. If they slipped on the trail, the fall might kill them, but if they didn't get out of its way, the avalanche sure as hell would.

Longarm waved an arm over his head to get Julia's attention. "Run! Run, damnit!"

She looked back and forth between the avalanche and the two men who were still fighting for their lives.

Then instead of turning to flee, she darted forward, heading for Galloway and Hawley.

Longarm bit back a curse as he saw what Julia was doing. She picked up a rock as she ran toward the two men. Hawley had managed to get on top, and he was slowly forcing the barrel of his gun toward Galloway.

Julia lifted the rock above her head and brought it crashing down on the back of Hawley's skull. The unexpected blow knocked Hawley forward, spilling him off of Galloway. The gun flew from his hand.

Longarm saw all that as he reached the bottom of the trail. He waved Chamberlain past him, telling the doctor to run like hell. Then he dashed toward Julia, Galloway, and Hawley.

Hawley rolled over and came up on his hands and knees, shaking his head groggily as Julia tried to help Galloway to his feet. Longarm reached her side and bent down to grasp Galloway's other arm. Together, they hauled the former outlaw to his feet. The rumble of the avalanche was so loud now that the earth shook.

Hawley spotted his fallen revolver and lunged for it. Longarm fired the Winchester one-handed. The slug kicked up dirt between Hawley and the gun and made him jerk back.

"Leave it! We gotta get out of here!"

To illustrate his point, Longarm shoved Julia and Galloway toward the mouth of the canyon. Julia hung on to Galloway's arm and kept him moving. They broke into a stumbling run.

Hawley lurched to his feet and stared wildly at Longarm. The rain plastered his hair to his scalp and ran down his face.

"The gold!"

"Forget the gold!" Longarm glanced at the two outlaws who had tried to pull the bags from under the overhang. They both lay still now, sprawled in grotesque attitudes of death. The rattlers had finally let go of them and slithered back up into their den. "You can't get it!"

"I can! I won't leave it!"

Hawley turned and ran toward the overhang.

Longarm let him go. The man was mad, mad with the lust for gold. The packhorses were gone, having stampeded back out of the canyon without anyone to hold their reins. Hawley didn't have any way to haul the gold out of here, even without an avalance and a nest of rattlesnakes to worry about.

But it was time for Longarm to save his own hide. He turned and ran as hard as he could after Julia and Galloway.

He heard a scream and glanced back once. Hawley had managed to pull one heavy canvas bag out of the cache. He staggered along the floor of the canyon with the bag cradled in his arms and a snake dangling from the back of one hand by its fangs.

That glimpse of Hawley was all Longarm got. Then the leading edge of the avalanche came crashing down, blotting out Noah Hawley and the snake and the gold as if none of them had ever been there.

Longarm kept running like the end of the world was right on his heels.

And that was pretty much what it amounted to . . .

"If I hadn't seen Hawley with one of those bags, I might've been tempted to think that you lied to him about where that gold was hidden, old son."

Longarm puffed on one of the cigars from the desk in the marshal's office as he watched Dr. Chamberlain wrapping bandages around Galloway's torso. Hawley's last shot had glanced off one of Galloway's ribs, breaking it and leaving a nasty wound, but one that wasn't going to prove fatal, according to the doctor. Della McKittredge stood next to Galloway with a hand on his shoulder and a worried look on her face.

"It was the truth. I wasn't going to take any chances with Della's life, or Jasper's. Right then, I didn't give a damn about the gold." Galloway looked over at Della. "To tell you the truth, I still don't."

Longarm grinned around the cigar. "I don't imagine Uncle Sam will feel the same way. Question is, will the government think it's worth the trouble to go in and dig it out from under that avalanche?"

"You're going to tell them where it is?"

Longarm perched his hip on a corner of the desk. "Got

to. It was my job to find Ed Galloway and to find that gold."

Everybody in the room turned disapproving frowns toward Longarm. The marshal's office was crowded. Julia Foster was there, along with Barney Schmidt, Josh Willard, and Arnie Davidson, the café owner sporting one arm in a sling from being shot when the outlaws broke Hawley out of jail.

Julia stepped forward. "You can't do that! You can't turn Marshal Ryan in, Custis. It just wouldn't be fair."

"Aye, he's a good man." Davidson's rumbling voice sounded almost like the thunder that had filled the air earlier.

"We don't care what he did before." That was Barney Schmidt. "He's the best lawman Warhorse has ever had. And he's our friend."

Longarm took the cigar out of his mouth and blew a smoke ring. "Actually, I ought to arrest all of you for interfering with a federal officer in the performance of his duties. I ain't forgot about how you jumped me, knocked me out, and held me prisoner."

He didn't mention the things that had gone on between him and Julia during that interval, but he could tell from the sudden flush that spread over her face that she was thinking about them.

Chamberlain had finished bandaging Galloway's injuries. Galloway patted the hand that Della still rested on his shoulder, then moved it and stepped toward Longarm with a grim, resolute expression on his rugged face.

"There's no need for you to arrest anybody except me, Marshal. I'll go with you willingly and face whatever justice the court wants to mete out."

Della took his hand and faced Longarm, too. "But it won't *be* justice. Whatever debt Pat owes to society, he's paid by taking such good care of this town the past two years. And if that's not enough, Marshal, think about all he could do for Warhorse in the future if you just . . . just . . ."

"Lie to my boss? Falsify an official report?"

Galloway shook his head. "I won't ask you to do that." He looked around the room at the others. "And nobody else here will, either."

Della looked anguished. "Pat . . ."

"Let Marshal Long do his job, Della."

A strained silence fell over the office as Longarm puffed on the cigar, tugged at his earlobe, and ran his thumbnail along the line of his jaw. He wasn't thinking quite as deeply as he appeared to be, since he had already made up his mind, but they didn't have to know that.

"I came here to recover the gold and to see that Cullen Johnson's murderer was brought to justice. Well, I know where the gold is—it's buried under tons of rock—and poor old Cullen's killer is buried right there with it. So I reckon my job here is done."

Hope sprang to life in Della's eyes, but Galloway still looked wary. "Just what do you mean by that, Marshal?"

"I mean the charges against Ed Galloway are wiped off the books as long as he's dead. You think he's gonna stay that way?"

Della clutched Marshal Pat Ryan's uninjured arm as he nodded. "I think you can count on that."

Julia hurried forward and threw her arms around Longarm's neck. The other townspeople crowded around him to shake his hand and slap him on the back.

Billy Vail might not understand what he had just done, thought Longarm . . . but on the other hand, the old hell-raiser just might. Billy had been a lawman for a long time, and any lawman worth his salt knew that sometimes justice and the law weren't exactly the same thing.

A few minutes later, when they were done thanking him, Longarm stepped out onto the porch. Julia followed him.

The rain had stopped again, and this time it looked like the storm had moved on for good. The clouds were breaking up, with patches of blue sky and sunshine visible overhead.

"The arroyo's flooded again, Custis. It'll take a while for the water to go down."

Longarm nodded. "I know."

"So you're stuck here in Warhorse for the time being, right?"

"Looks like it."

"Good." Julia leaned her head against his shoulder as his arm went around her. "Because there are a lot of things in that book I told you about that we haven't tried yet."

Longarm chuckled. Looked like it was going to be a beautiful day.

Watch for

LONGARM AND THE ONE-ARMED BANDIT

the 380ᵗʰ novel in the exciting LONGARM
series from Jove

Coming in July!

GIANT-SIZED ADVENTURE FROM AVENGING ANGEL LONGARM.

BY TABOR EVANS

2006 Giant Edition:

LONGARM AND THE OUTLAW EMPRESS

2007 Giant Edition:

LONGARM AND THE GOLDEN EAGLE SHOOT-OUT

2008 Giant Edition:

LONGARM AND THE VALLEY OF SKULLS

2009 Giant Edition:

LONGARM AND THE LONE STAR TRACKDOWN

penguin.com/actionwesterns

DON'T MISS A YEAR OF

Slocum Giant
by
Jake Logan

Slocum Giant 2004:
Slocum in the Secret Service

Slocum Giant 2005:
Slocum and the Larcenous Lady

Slocum Giant 2006:
Slocum and the Hanging Horse

Slocum Giant 2007:
Slocum and the Celestial Bones

Slocum Giant 2008:
Slocum and the Town Killers

Slocum Giant 2009:
Slocum's Great Race

M457AS0409

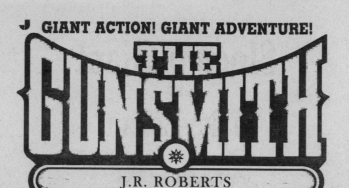

GIANT ACTION! GIANT ADVENTURE!

THE GUNSMITH

J.R. ROBERTS

Little Sureshot And
The Wild West Show
(Gunsmith Giant #9)

Dead Weight
(Gunsmith Giant #10)

Red Mountain
(Gunsmith Giant #11)

The Knights of Misery
(Gunsmith Giant #12)

The Marshal from Paris
(Gunsmith Giant #13)

Lincoln's Revenge
(Gunsmith Giant #14)

penguin.com/actionwesterns

M455AS0509